W9-ADW-590

TWO OF US

TWO OF US

Leslie Stewart

Arlington Books
King St, St James's
London

TWO OF US

First published 1989 by
Arlington Books (Publishers) Ltd
15–17 King Street, London SW1

British Library Cataloguing-in-Publication Data

Stewart, Leslie, 1949–
Two of us.
I. Title
823'.914 [F]

ISBN 0–85140–749–8

Typeset by J&L Composition Ltd, Filey
Printed and bound in Great Britain by
Billing & Sons Ltd, Worcester

For Thomas and Sarah.
For my Mother and my Father.
For Andrew, Jenny, Hannah and Allison.
For Paula.

For Roger, Andrew, Graham and Peter
and everyone who worked on the film.
And for Michael Richmond

A local authority shall not—(a) intentionally promote homosexuality or publish material with the intention of promoting homosexuality; (b) promote the teaching in any maintained school of the acceptability of homosexuality as a pretended family relationship.
(Clause 28 Subsection 2A—1, Local Government Act 1988)

This land of such dear souls, this dear, dear land,
Dear for her reputation through the world,
Is now leased out—I die pronouncing it –
Like to a tenement or pelting farm.
England bound in with the triumphant sea,
Whose rocky shore beats back the envious siege
Of watery Neptune, is now bound in with shame,
With inky blots, and rotten parchment bonds.
That England that was wont to conquer others,
Hath made a shameful conquest of itself.

William Shakespeare, *Richard II*, c. 1595

Prologue

One Saturday night I went to a barbecue with Matthew at a pub in Epping. We got there too late for the food, which was just as well as I didn't much like the look of the left-overs.

Todd was there, drunk and dancing in the garden. A few weeks before, he'd wanted me to listen to a cassette he'd just bought. I had to listen to it in his car.

'It always sounds better in a car,' he said.

We went for a drive and ended up at a microlight field near Harlow. I said wouldn't it be wonderful if we just drove onto the field, accelerated past all those weird flying-machines, and took off. On the way back Todd stopped the car at a ditch at the side of a field and showed me the rusty wreck of a van. 'My dad used to drive one of those. I remember going in it with him when I was little,' he told me. 'He just dumped it one day. This could be it,' he said.

The music at the disco was good but distorted and the only real excitement was being asked to dance by two very pretty girls who were trying it on. It didn't have to be us, we just looked available. Matthew and I politely declined. They tried to persuade us by using all the talent at their disposal. I even got my thigh stroked.

Outside, where Todd was dancing, someone had put out bales of straw so that people could sit and cuddle and kiss and lie with each other. All the girls (and they were girls) appeared to be in charge; the boys (and they were boys) appeared anxious. *Will she? Won't she? Will I get to drop me drawers before they drop the bomb?* There was a lot of kissing. I just watched. I watched and I thought about kissing Matthew. I thought about how his hair fell across his face when he kissed me.

I loved Matthew and he loved me. But we loved each other differently. Maybe he was more involved, more in love. He hated endings, he told me. I was happy to love him for however long it would last. I never really thought about it ending.

I watched him at the barbecue that night. I watched him chatting up the girls, and being chatted up. But he never danced with them, instead he would come back to me and sit next to me. We didn't talk much. You can only say 'I love you' so many times a night.

They didn't touch either; that would have been dangerous. The only sympathy they would have got would have been from the sky and the stars and the romance of the night—never much of a defence.

Todd came over with a pint and a girl, whose name he'd forgotten, and said he had to go. He handed Phil his pint and squeezed the girl, who giggled. They rushed off towards the car park.

By the time Matthew and Phil had decided it was time to leave the dancing had become desperate. Pissed boys groped at last dance chances, watched by tired bouncers, whose faces flickered on and off in the colour strobes of the disco lights.

Romance!

'Matthew, I love you.' Phil said, not whispering but loud above the music.

'Not here, Phil.' Matthew laughed but he was clearly worried. 'Not here. Please.'

'They'll think we're pissed. Come on, let's dance.'

'No.'

Once, after school, Phil and Matthew met in a shopping arcade. Phil ran up to Matthew and kissed him.

'What are you doing?' Matthew asked as he pushed Phil away. 'We're being watched.'

'So what?' said Phil. 'Footballers do it, don't they? Thousands watch them. Millions.'

They made a game of it then and chased each other through the shoppers.

Romance.

1

Matthew waited outside the swimming pool as Phil and Sharon walked past the squash centre and crossed the car park. It was a hot day and the air shimmered around the parked cars.

Sharon saw Matthew first. She waved. 'He gives me the creeps,' she said.

'He's alright.' Phil remembered the barbecue and remembered not to tell Sharon about it.

'Yeah?'

'Yes.'

Sharon had missed school that day because of what she called women's problems. This was a catch-all excuse that invited no questions or further investigation. Women were understanding, and men? Well, men were men. She waited round the corner and out of sight for Phil to come out of school. She waited like a wife waits at a suburban railway station.

Sharon was pretty and had the sort of body that made swimming with her as much an exercise in voyeurism as anything else. She was soft in the right places and firm where boredom hadn't yet got hold. Phil had been going out with her for about a year, ever since his fifteenth birthday when she gave him a present on her mother's sofa. It wasn't anything too rude and didn't require unwrapping, it was simply the wettest kiss he'd ever had.

Matthew looked good in the pool. They all watched him, boys and girls alike. He was well built, his body tapered, as only a swimmer's does, from broad, muscled shoulders to a waist as slim as a girl's. His sandy hair was bleached as though by the sun. Phil was positively fragile and waif-like compared to Matthew. Wet only to his ankles, he sat on the pool's edge between Sharon and her friend Vera, who was always there on a Friday afternoon. They all wanted to be like Matthew, or to be him. A high-board diver, he was a star and he knew it. He could swim as well as he could dive. He probably gave Sharon the creeps because she was attracted to him. They all were in their own ways. Matthew was beautiful.

Later, whilst Phil and Matthew were in the showers, a group of fourth formers from Phil's school came into the changing room.

'I ain't going in there with him,' one of them announced, waving a limp wrist at Matthew.

'Phil,' another called. 'Sharon know about you and him, does she?'

His mates laughed. Phil looked across at Matthew, who kept his face turned to the wall. He's frightened, Phil thought. Matthew's bloody frightened.

The fourth years, having made their point and

established their masculinity walked into the changing area singing: '*Here we go, here we go, here we go . . .*'

'Matthew?' Phil's voice was soft with concern. He wanted to hold Matthew and tell him that he loved him. 'They've gone.'

'Piss off,' Matthew said without turning from the wall.

Not many days later, eighteen sixth-formers sat at their desks and listened, half amused, as Mr Cross, a sociology teacher, attempted a classroom discussion on sexual orientation.

'Homos,' Sarah offered from her seat next to Phil at the back of the class.

'Queers,' another added.

'Pooves,' Mr Cross suggested.

'Queens,' chimed yet another happy little voice.

'Lesbians. Dykes.' Mr Cross kept the game going. 'Girls do it as well, you know.'

Sarah started to laugh. 'How do they do it, sir. I mean, what do they use?'

'Don't be silly, Sarah.' Mr Cross turned to the blackboard and wrote the words: 'Gays, Perverts, Deviants' with an attack and an energy that sent little clouds of chalk-dust flying into the air. 'Hitler killed them. The Church condemned them. Civilized society persecutes them,' he told the class.

(Is it possible for a civilized society to persecute anyone?)

'You can get nicked for it an' all,' Dennis the Greek reckoned.

'You can indeed.' Mr Cross seized on Dennis's contribution to the discussion with relish. 'Homosexuality can cost you your job, your friends, your family. It can even cost you your freedom.' He returned to the blackboard and wrote the slogan ONE IN TEN. 'Recent surveys suggest that one teenager in ten is gay.'

Dennis got to his feet. 'Alright, you lot. There's twenty of us in here. Play the white man, guys. Own up, both of you. Who is it, then?' He'd have to start shaving in a few months. Soft, dark down covered his cheeks and jaw, and he already had what could pass for a moustache. Another thing about Dennis—his eyes were too far apart and his top lip twitched whenever he was trying to be flash. What Dennis needed, Phil thought, was a good screwing. He needed a small humiliation, a little death. Dennis laughed at his own joke.

'Sit down, boy.' Mr Cross was weary now. This was not how it was supposed to be.

'Shut up, Dennis,' said Sarah. 'We had one once, sir,' she added. 'His name was Matthew, but he left.'

'What you mean is that he didn't fancy you,' Dennis said.

'Don't be a wally,' said Sarah. It crossed Phil's mind as they bickered that maybe Sarah should screw Dennis.

'Sit down, Dennis.'

'I don't feel safe, sir.'

'Then you'd better sit down, hadn't you?'

It started to rain. Phil watched the rain-drops hit the window. The world outside was washed into an oily blur. Phil screwed up his eyes and imagined being almost blind, able only to differentiate between light and dark. The thought of a world where no shape was fixed, where nothing was set, and the only definitions were whatever he understood them to be was comforting. He made a mental note never again to give money to the blind.

Mr Cross sat on the edge of his desk and started to read to the class. 'When I realized I was homosexual, the first thing I did was to sit down and cry. I wept for myself, but mostly I cried because I didn't conform. I couldn't be this way because it just wasn't right. I wondered why the same sex attracted me.'

'Because he was a pervert, that's why,' Dennis muttered.

'Shut up, Dennis!' said Vi in a flash of anger so sudden it surprised even her.

'Thank you, Vi.' Mister Cross was grateful for the interruption.

'Well I think it's sad.' Vi blushed. She was a chubby, mouse of a girl and embarrassed by the attention she'd drawn on herself.

The bell rang signalling the end of the lesson. The rain continued to smack against the window.

Phil wanted to cry then. He just wanted to sit there by the window and cry. He thought about kissing Sharon and the rudeness of her breasts. And he thought about Matthew.

Phil looked away from the window. 'You got a minute, sir?'

'Only just.' Mr Cross and Phil were alone in the classroom. 'It's my night for being grown-up.' Mr Cross explained.

'Sorry?'

'I'm baby-sitting. I'm doing the ironing. Do you want me to go on?'

'No,' Phil said.

'Well?'

'How do you know if you are?'

'Are what?'

'You know.'

'Ah.' Mister Cross sighed and continued to pack his papers and his books into his briefcase. 'One in ten. Work it out for yourself.'

'Seriously, though.'

'Are you worried about it?'

'I've got a friend.'

'I see.'

'Matthew.' It was all quick-fire; too quick, as though they were playing a word game.

'The dreaded Matthew, eh?'

'He's alright.'

'But he's worried?' Mr Cross had all the questions.

'I don't know.'

'You've got a girlfriend, haven't you?'

Phil wanted to ask what exactly a girlfriend was. 'Sort of,' he answered.

'But?'

'Of course I've got a girlfriend. Sharon.'

'If something really is bothering you, or your friend. . . If you are confused about certain feelings, you can get help.'

'Like what?'

'Counselling. Help.' Mr Cross snapped his briefcase shut and edged towards the door. He was going to be late. 'There are people you can talk to. Experts.'

'What sort of experts?'

'You can see a doctor.'

'A doctor?'

'To put his mind at rest, your friend's mind.' If he could only get to a phone, he thought, he could call home and explain. Then he'd have time. He thought about his wife and the anger that lurked beneath her steely understanding.

'I just want to know more about it, that's all,' Phil said.

Mr Cross looked at his watch and reached for the door handle. 'It might help straighten him out, if that's what's needed.' He was beginning to panic. Not only was he going to be late but he was also caught up in a reality that nobody had prepared him for.

'Maybe I'll get a book out of the library, eh?'

'You do that.'

'Thanks.'

'Look, any other time you need to talk, you know where to find me.'

'Baby-sitting.'

'I'm sorry.' He was. He was truly sorry.

'Yeah.'

Flowers. Doesn't matter what the season, there are always flowers in London. If they don't grow them, they sell them; if they don't sell them, they buy them; if they don't buy them, they receive them.

Romance. *Ro-bleeding-mance.*

'You can kiss me on the cheek if you like,' Sharon offered as she and Phil passed a flower stall.

'No thanks.'

'What's the matter?' Sharon didn't really mind whether Phil kissed her or not. This was something she was offering, not something she was asking for.

'I've got to go and see a doctor, haven't I?'

'You serious?'

'Course I'm serious.'

'What's wrong then?'

'It's personal. A personal matter, Sharon.'

'You can tell me.'

He made her promise not to tell anyone. She promised, and the promise of a secret, a shared confidence, made her feel a small rush of love for

Phil, her boyfriend. He wasn't particularly handsome or stylish or extraordinary in any way. But she loved him. She probably loved him much as her mother loved her father. He was comfortable to be with and, in the main, didn't give her a hard time.

'I've got to have it cut off,' he said. 'Amputated.'

'Have what cut off?'

'*It*, Sharon. They'll probably put me in a private ward because of the nature of the operation. I'll get counselling, of course. You'll need some as well, won't you?'

'*It?*'

Phil nodded solemnly then looked down at his crotch. 'Will you send me flowers?'

At the disco on Friday night Sharon and Phil danced in the back room of the Spread Eagle. Trestle tables had been pushed up against the walls leaving the floor clear for the dancing. Matthew was there at one of the tables watching Phil and Sharon and half listening to a man in his mid-twenties, unashamedly made-up and girl-mannered, who was sitting next to him.

Sharon looked over Phil's shoulder at Matthew. 'Do you love me?' she asked.

'I don't know, do I?' Phil pulled her closer to him. 'Of course I love you.'

'Your friend's here,' she kissed Phil on the cheek, 'Talking to that queer feller from the bar.'

Phil spun her round and looked across at Matthew, who laughed. The queer feller from the bar shared the joke. Phil felt a sudden need to get out of the room; to get away from Sharon, Matthew and the queer feller from the bar.

'I'm going outside,' he whispered in Sharon's ear. He pulled away from her and walked quickly to the door. She followed him. *Sod him. Sod it. Sod the lot of them.*

Outside, where the air was cool and chilled the sweat under his shirt, Phil waited. He knew Sharon would come angrily through the door. That was the thing about Sharon, he always knew what she would do next.

'Phil.' She was angry.

'What?'

'What's the matter?'

'I'll take you home if you like.'

'I don't have to be home for hours yet.'

'You go back in then.' Right now Phil didn't really care what she did.

'On me own? Go back in there on me own?' Sharon didn't ask questions, she fired them. 'Unaccompanied? What are they all going to think? I'm meant to be with you.'

'It's all couples, Sharon. They're all practising at being married.'

'You know what? You're odd, mate. We're a couple.' Phil noticed the make-up around her eyes as though for the first time. It was too black, too heavy; her lipstick, rather than complementing the shape of her lips, distorted them.

'I don't fancy it.' He couldn't look at her anymore, not tonight.

'You're strange.' He imagined the lipstick changing shape as she spoke the words. 'I reckon you're weird.'

'I'm not. Promise.'

'Well I ain't standing here all night.' She rubbed her arms against the cold.

'I'm sorry.' He remembered seeing a middle-aged man lying on the pavement after a fight. He was lying where they were standing now surrounded by a mob of grotesque drunks. He remembered the blood around the man's mouth and his chillingly white teeth shining through his swollen lips. 'I'm sorry.' He wanted to say more. He wanted to explain about the mascara and the lipstick.

'Yeah,' Sharon said, then she went back into the disco.

Phil turned to the door as it swung shut. 'I'm not weird. One hundred percent, straight up, absolutely, completely unweird, Sharon.'

Romance.

Matthew watched Sharon as she returned to the disco and pushed her way through the dancers.

'You on you're own then?' he asked as she passed his table.

'Looks like it, doesn't it?'

Matthew got to his feet. 'Good night,' he said.

Sharon stared after him as he crossed the floor and left the room. 'I know where he's off to. Bastard,' she announced to anyone who cared to listen.

The queer feller from the bar turned to her and shrugged. Sharon noticed the glitter around his eyes as he looked up at her. She wanted to hug him then. She didn't know why, she just wanted to put her arms around him and hold him. He appeared to her to be as lonely as she felt. He, for his part, felt sorry for her. He was just another floozie who once shone at snooker, and he felt sorry for Sharon. One day he'd write it all down. One day. Whenever he tried to start, he'd lose his nerve. Instead of committing his life to paper he would make a list of things to do. Always on the list would be a reminder to write it all down.

'You alright?' Sharon asked him.

The queer feller was fine.

2

That night, after the disco and the words with Sharon, I took the long way home. I wanted to walk and for once I didn't wish I'd had a Ford XR3 Cabriolet to cruise the night in.

Matthew caught up with me at the corner of Egremont Street, where Todd's brother had his video shop.

'You're causing me grief, do you know that?' I said.

'Grief?' he asked.

'Grief,' I said. Then he put his arms around me and kissed me.

He walked me home but said he didn't want to come in, which was okay because I didn't much fancy the idea of having to make polite conversation with him and my mum. If he did come in, I would have wanted to sit close to him, I would have wanted to sit with him as lovers do. It wouldn't have been on, not over a cup of tea, not with mum there. We said goodnight and I watched after him until he'd turned the corner at the end of our street.

My home was a maisonette built in the early seventies. My parents had painted the walls of the living room orange and green in memory of the sixties, their decade. A paper lamp-shade hung from the ceiling. Its pattern—I think it was Chinese—had faded away long before dad left home. Plants still in their plastic pots drank from saucers wherever you looked. Mum liked plants. She didn't talk to them or anything like that, but she said they were good company. The three-piece suite was well worn and of a style that was so fashionable when it was bought that it never really stood a chance. Mum said that it was almost collectable.

The smell of frying was in all the rooms. It was a smell I loved. It was the only smell I knew that told me I was home. Other people's homes smelled of aerosolled lilies of the valley, or of disinfectant, or of dog-farts. Sharon's home smelled of nail-varnish. Mine smelled of chips. Mum was watching television when I got in.

'Mum?'

'Yes, dear?' She said this without looking up at me. She was a pretty woman was my mum. She still is.

'Do you think I'm weird?' I asked her.

'What's weird when it's at home?' She turned away from the telly, looked me over then turned back to the telly again.

I walked across the the room and stood between her and the set.'Do you think there's anything odd about me?' I asked her.

'I never did like that jacket,' she said. 'Do you mind, I'm trying to watch this.'

I moved out of her way. A woman on television was dying in a hospital bed whilst a man was telling her he loved her and that he wanted to marry her.

'Had a row with Sharon, have you?' she asked, having already worked out the answer.

'Sort of.'

'A tiff,' mum said. 'We used to have tiffs when I was your age.'

Then I started to cry. I could feel my eyes getting wet and when I looked down the floor seemed closer than usual. I felt little again.

'Come here.' Mum patted the sofa.

'Why?' I asked. I wanted to sit with her but I wanted her to make it easy for me.

'Because I need a cuddle.'

I sat next to her and let her cuddle me.

The woman on the telly was almost dead now. She reached out across the sheets to touch the man's hand. He grabbed her hand and squeezed it.

'Silly old films, eh?' Mum was trying to be brave. 'Bring out the tissues, your dad used to say. It'll be alright, Phil. It all works out in the end. It's called the formula. A lot of tears, more music and everyone gets what they deserve in the end.'

Then the woman on the telly died.

The pool was almost deserted. It was 'diving hour', a time reserved for those who had more serious things on their minds than horseplay. Matthew stood on the high-board preparing to dive. Below him spray from a hose-pipe played on the pool's surface disturbing the water just enough to give him an idea of where it started. Phil watched from the pool's edge.

Upstairs in the cafeteria Sharon and Vera were sitting at a table with a view of the pool. They had a bun and a can of coke each.

'Where's Phil then?' Vera asked as Sharon watched Matthew spring from the high-board.

'Learning to fly,' she said.

'That's nice. I can't even swim.' Vera sighed.

Down below them, Matthew surfaced and swam across the pool to Phil with an effortless yet powerful stroke.

'He's tasty, isn't he?' Vera said. She took a bite out of her bun.

'No chance,' Sharon whispered. 'He doesn't like girls.'

'Pity.' Vera thought of the waste of it all. 'No harm in looking, though.' She tried to imagine Matthew and another boy holding hands. She pictured them listening to music in a car parked in a lay-by. 'Does he dress up?'

'I don't know.'

'He'd look nice in a frock.'

'He doesn't wear bloody frocks.'

'What does Phil see in him then?'

'I don't know.' Vera's interest in Matthew was

beginning to irritate Sharon. 'Can't we talk about something else?' she pleaded.

'Are you alright, you and Phil?'

'Brilliant,' Sharon said. 'I'm alright. I don't know about him, though.' She moved the straw up and down in her coke can until froth bubbled out of the end and spilled on her fingers.

'It's a phase, Sharon,' Vera offered. 'He's having a crush. He's a late developer. He's trying to be modern, that's all.' She craned forward to get a better look at Matthew and Phil in the pool. 'It could be tragic though.'

'What do you mean?' Sharon didn't like the sound of the word *tragic*; to her it meant newspaper headlines, news-flashes, whispered gossip—it meant victims.

'It's two out of the game, isn't it?' Vera hissed. 'Two less for me to get ambitious about.'

'You're evil, Vera. Do you know that?'

Vera winked and turned back to the window to look at the boys down in the pool.

In the changing room afterwards, when they were both naked, Phil watched Matthew under the shower.

'Something wrong?' Matthew asked.

'No,' Phil said and stepped in beside him.

Later, much later, long after they'd washed the chlorine from their eyes and their hair, Matthew touched Phil. He put a hand to Phil's face and let it fall to his chest. Phil thought of Sharon in the women's changing rooms with Vera: Big Vera, who never really stood a chance in the games they (we) all played. She would never have a surplus of admirers, but the few she would have would really love her. He thought about the mysteries of women's changing rooms. What did they talk about? What life—changing decisions were arrived at by the minute in that secret, steamy world? Did they discuss breast enlargements and footwear? Did they wash and dry and dress in silence with thoughts only of who they might wash and dry and dress for next? Or did they touch like Matthew was touching him?

'It's alright,' Matthew whispered. 'It's alright.'

'I know it's alright.' Phil moved closer to Matthew and kissed him, first on the corner of his mouth and then on his lips.

They didn't talk anymore. They just stood there under the showers listening to the water as it drummed on their bodies and around their feet like a South American carnival. The rhythms crossed and changed and filled their heads. Phil wanted Matthew to touch him again and at that moment, at the precise point when Phil needed Matthew's touch, the sound of a locker door being slammed into place warned them that just a few feet away the real world was still crashing dangerously about.

Romance.

Matthew turned to the wall and started to wash

all over again. Phil lifted his face to the water and let it run into his mouth.

When they came out of the showers the changing room was deserted. A black canvas shoe sat forlornly in a puddle and a pair of electric blue trousers shared a hook with a thread-bare towel.

Phil grabbed a wire clothes basket from the wooden, slatted bench that ran the length of one of the walls. Shaped like a human torso, it had a coat-hanger for shoulders and a basket for a belly. 'Hello, Sharon,' Phil said, holding it as he would someone he was about to kiss. 'I've got some good news. You'll never guess. I'm one in ten. Bingo! I've won the pools. I'm twice as lucky as most and proud of it. It's quite simple, really. I fancy you,' he turned to Matthew, who was drying his hair. 'And I fancy him. Good, eh? Thought that would please you. That's what mates are for, isn't it? Let's all go out together and celebrate my win.' He considered Matthew for a long moment. 'You do like me, don't you?' Phil asked him. 'It is important.'

'Are you really going to tell her?'

'I'll find a way.' Phil hung the basket on one of the hooks.

'Why don't you just split up with her?'

'Because I don't want to, that's why,' Phil snapped and instantly regretted it. Matthew buried his head in his towel and rubbed away furiously at his hair.

'What happens next, Matthew?'

Homosexuality can cost you your job, your friends.
Poof! Poof! Poof!
Your friend's here, talking to that queer bloke from the pub.
Sharon know about you and him, does she?
Do you love me?
Nancy boy.
You're odd, mate.
Queer.
I reckon you're weird.
What's it like doing it with blokes?

Upstairs, in the cafeteria, Sharon was becoming impatient. There was a whole world of Phils out there. There were better things to do than to just sit here watching the cream die on her bun. 'I ain't waiting much longer.'

'I had a feller once,' said Vera, surprised by the memory.

'So?'

'That's it really.' Vera shrugged off the disappointment of it all and sighed.

Romance.

When we went up to the cafeteria Sharon and Vera pretended not to see us. This was it, then. I was going to tell her; my big moment and she pretended not to see me. Matthew wanted to go home. He wanted to sneak off and leave me to it. 'Sod that,' I told him. 'We're in this together, mate.'

We got to their table and I sat next to Sharon. Vera moved over for Matthew. I think she fancied him.

'Well?' Sharon wanted to know what was going on.

'Hello, Sharon,' I said. 'Meet Matthew, my boyfriend. Matthew, meet Sharon, my girlfriend.' That didn't go down too well.

'I didn't come here to mess about, Phil,' Sharon said. 'I thought we were going to talk,' Then she got up. I couldn't see her because she was standing behind me, but I knew she was looking at Vera, looking for moral support. I winked at Vera and she kicked me under the table.

'You're not very funny,' Sharon snapped at the back of my head. Then I heard her walk away from the table.

Vera got up. 'You're a worm,' she told me. Somehow, though, she managed to find a smile for Matthew as she squeezed past him. Vera is a tart.

We waited for them to leave the cafeteria; me listening to their footsteps, Matthew watching them. 'That was a bit prattish,' he said when they'd gone.

'What do you know about it?' I asked.

'I know a prat when I see one.'

'I told her, didn't I?' I'd done what he'd wanted me to do. I'd owned up, I'd come out to my girlfriend. And he called me a prat.

'She doesn't like you, Matthew. She thinks you're a creep.'

'So?'

'So she smiles and she waves and, when you can't hear her, she calls you a creep.'

Matthew shrugged. I looked hard at him and there was no warmth there, nothing. I tried a smile, I tried to make a joke of it all, but he just got up and walked out. I looked down at the pool and saw a fat man on the high-board. He was on tip-toes and fully stretched. I watched him dive then I got up and left.

Phil saw Sharon the next day. They'd arranged to meet long before the fracas in the pool cafeteria. Now, neither knew whether the other would turn up.

Sharon waited at the entrance to the municipal tennis courts. Though the courts were concrete, the surrounding area was grassed and even boasted bushes and beds of flowers, which managed to survive the poisons belched out by the steady stream of traffic that passed within yards of them. They had adapted to the environment they found themselves in and would probably have died of boredom in a place more suitable to their kind.

Phil saw Sharon long before she saw him. He could turn and run if he wanted to and she would never know he'd come. She would feel stood-up and humiliated. Only Phil, his pride intact (for Sharon had, after all, turned up), would know the truth. But that wasn't the game anyone was about to play.

'I'm sorry about yesterday. Okay?' Phil, embarrassed at the memory of it all, muttered as they walked across one of the tennis courts.

'I felt a right idiot,' Sharon explained. 'I was really embarrassed, what with Vera and him being there.'

'Me and all.'

'That's alright, then.' Sharon brightened up. She smoothed her skirt under her and sat on a bench at the side of the court.

'I want to explain.'

'Don't bother.'

'But I want to.'

'I don't want to hear about it.' She was beginning to feel angry again. All she wanted from Phil now was a kiss, a fumbled attempt at a grope and the reassurance implicit in such an encounter.

'It's important. And you're my best mate, right?'

'I'm your girlfriend. And you're my bloke. I just don't want to hear about him.'

'I made a joke about it and it came out wrong. I didn't mean to take the piss.'

'I don't want to know, Phil.'

They sat in silence for a long time staring at the court. They were like strangers caught on the same bench waiting for a game to start.

'I fancy him,' Phil said, staring fixedly at the net. 'I'm gay.'

'You're a prat.'

'Not gay then, bi-sexual.'

'That's just modern. What do you mean you fancy him?'

'Just that.'

'Like with me?'

'Yes.' Then he started to lose it. He felt the logic of it falling away from him; the sense of it all was beginning to crack. 'I don't know.'

'What do you mean you don't know?'

'It's different. But I fancy him.'

'You want to get help, mate.' Sharon was feeling sick. The weirdness of what was happening made her dizzy, light-headed. Anything could be said now, there could be no more surprises. This was dangerous territory for a sixteen-year-old whose expectations of life were encapsulated in and daily reaffirmed by what passed for the norm, or by what she perceived as the norm: American/Australian television soap operas, macho violence, prams, push-chairs and shopping trolleys; Radio 1, disasters in hot countries, tragedies nearer home, the wedding of an older cousin, the birth of yet another royal, puppies, rows at home and clean knickers. Here she was on a bench with a stranger watching an empty tennis court. 'Have you done it with him?' she asked. If he said *he had,* would she want to know more? What did they do? How did they do it? What does it feel like doing it with a bloke?

'No,' Phil answered. They'd kissed and touched and even masturbated each other, but they hadn't what Sharon would call *done it.*

'Why not?'

'I don't know.'

'Do you still want to do it with me?'

'Of course I do.'

'You're sick!' she jumped up from the bench and turned on him. 'D'you know that? You're a head-case. You're sick. Bloody, sodding sick. You're a poofter.'

'That doesn't mean anything, Sharon.'

'It bloody does.'

'I'm not a poofter.'

Sharon walked away then. Phil watched her go and made no attempt to call her back or to follow her. He knew that he'd see her again. It was inconceivable that he wouldn't. She was part of his life; she was his steady girlfriend and had been for some time. A bust-up now was unthinkable. They needed each other. They needed still the security of whatever history they already had. They needed to share things: music, films, gossip, friends, parties, the fear of losing each other to someone else. He waited until she'd crossed the road then got up and went in search of a bush to pee behind.

Phil found it hard to sleep on Sunday night. He tried masturbating but soon lost interest. He imagined doing it with Matthew, then with Sharon. He toyed with the thought of all three of them together in a bed, but Sharon, though captive and malleable in Phil's fantasy, wouldn't put her heart into it. He thought about telling Sharon he was sorry and offering to marry her and then he thought about Matthew and how he would miss him. He tried imagining going steady with Matthew and never seeing Sharon again. He thought briefly of suicide but was put off by the mechanics of such an act. He prayed for sleep.

He woke early the next morning, early enough to wake his mother with a cup of tea. She was surprised at the treat.

'What's this in aid of?' she asked not ungratefully.

'Nothing,' Phil said, placing the cup on the bedside table. 'I couldn't sleep, that's all.' He sat on the edge of the bed and remembered being little and climbing in with his mother while she slept. He remembered the feel of her nightdress against his face as he lay next to her. Sometimes she would be naked and he would look at her under the sheets. She caught him once and told him off. The bedroom smelled the same now as it did then. The curtains hadn't been replaced and the carpet was worn in the same places. It was as if he'd just returned home after a long absence to find that nothing had changed.

'Mum?'

'Yes, dear?'

'Nothing really, just "mum".'

'Something the matter?' she asked.

'No, not really.' Phil said. 'I've got to go now.' He got off the bed and left the room.

'Thanks for the tea,' his mother called after him. She made a mental note to have a serious talk with Phil as soon as the opportunity arose. She would make him his favourite meal the next evening they were both home; maybe they would have a bottle of wine, and they would talk.

3

That morning, the morning I'd made tea for mum, I was one of the first to get to school. I went straight to my locker, which was in the corridor outside the classrooms. Written in lipstick on the inside of the door were the words: *BASTARD QUEER BUM BOY AIDS*. I slammed the locker door shut. Three boys and a girl were watching me. I hadn't noticed them before, they must have been hiding, waiting for me. For a moment I was frightened. I wanted Sharon to be there with me. I wanted to put my arms around her and kiss her—to show them.

'Sod off!' I yelled. 'Sod off! Sod off! Sod off!' They just walked away. I heard the girl laugh when she'd got round the corner. It was probably her lipstick. And she was only a soddin' third year.

I don't remember much about school that day, I kept thinking about Matthew and how much I was missing him. It was the first time I remember missing him.

I sat with Sharon at lunch. She didn't say much and I didn't tell her about the locker; I wanted to tell Matthew first. I thought it would be a bit like giving him a present. Sharon did say one thing that

I remember, she said that she'd spoken to Vera and that Vera liked me really and wanted us to be alright.

That afternoon Matthew was walking along the service road that led to the block of flats where he lived when he too was attacked. Unlike the attack on Phil, this was a physical assault, though no more or no less frightening. He was on his way back from his weekly visit to the job centre. The sound of children playing somewhere out of sight filled him with a sense of security.

As he approached the entrance to the flats a stone smacked into a parked car directly ahead of him. Another stone skidded across the tarmac and hit him on the ankle. A third stone gashed his head. Matthew spun round to search out the the danger but could see nobody. His attackers were well hidden. They were probably frightened. It's possible they were frightened of Matthew.

'Come on!' Matthew shouted. 'Come out here. Bastards!'

A milk bottle thrown by an invisible hand exploded at his feet. By the time Matthew had reached the relative safety of his home the left side of his face was warm with blood. He went into the bathroom and started to wash. That's where his father, a reasonable man, cornered him.

'What happened to you, then?' his father asked.

'I had an accident,' Matthew said continuing to wash away the blood.

'You don't have accidents, Matthew. You're good at games. Do you know what I mean?'

'No. As it happens, I don't.'

His father scattered a bundle of gay magazines across the floor. Caught on a bathroom floor between an angry father and a trapped boy, the young men on the magazine covers, once beautiful, became ridiculous.

'Your mother found them,' Matthew's father informed him. 'She found them hidden under your bed.'

'I'm sorry.'

'She left for work in tears.'

'I said I was sorry.'

'Is that all?'

'What else am I supposed to say?' Matthew wanted to be sick, or to wake up. Then a mad thought struck him—any second now his father would burst out laughing and declare the whole thing a good joke.

'It's not true, is it?'

'Dad?' He wanted to explain.

'They are yours, aren't they?'

'Yes.'

'I don't want to know,' his father shouted. 'You could have lied. You could have said you were keeping them for a friend.'

'But I wasn't.'

'Burn them. Chuck them. Not in our bin.' The anger had given way to a deep hurt. 'You could have lied.'

'I'm sorry,' Matthew said.

Matthew's father looked at him in silence. It struck him, for the first time, that his son was taller than him. He turned away and walked out of the bathroom.

Matthew would never again feel at ease in his own home. The space between him and his parents was there on the bathroom floor—jock-strapped and studded and as plastic as any cheap souvenir.

When Matthew told me about the hassle with his old man he sent the whole thing up. So he was caught with a couple of dirty magazines. So what? But then he told me about the stones and showed me the cut on his head. I told him about the words on my locker door. We'd both been done. It sort of brought us closer together.

That afternoon Matthew came round to my place. Mum was out for the day and as I wasn't going to be seeing Sharon until the evening, we knew we could be alone for few hours and forget about all the crap.

We sat close to each other on the sofa. Matthew was shivering and I asked him if he was cold.

'No, not cold,' he said.

'What then?' I asked. 'Do you want me to switch the fire on?' We had a gas fire with one of those wooden shelf things around it. When I was little, mum used to dry me in front of it after I'd had my bath. She still used it to dry her hair. She'd lie on her back and shake her hair out just inches from the fire. If I was there, I had to check that she didn't get too close.

'Just draw the curtains.' he said.

When I turned back from the window, Matthew had already taken off his shirt and was unbuckling his belt. He saw I was watching him and he stopped.

'It's alright,' I said.

Matthew and Phil lay pressed together on the sofa. There was a softness in the way Matthew had gathered Phil to him. Their physical differences made Phil appear vulnerable; a fledgling in a caring embrace.

They kissed and touched and stroked each other. They were gentle and unsure to start with, like the first time, like everybody's first time. Neither wanted to do the wrong thing, neither wanted to give in to the other's caresses. Then Matthew rose onto an elbow, kissed Phil hard on the mouth and began to make love to him with his hands and with his mouth. Phil gave in and forgot about Sharon and school and the graffiti on the locker door.

Later, after Matthew had gone, Phil sat naked in front of the small gas fire and tried to sort out his thoughts. He was happy, he knew that. He loved Matthew and he loved being with him. It didn't have to be sexual, they didn't have to be naked together, being together was enough. To know

Matthew, all he had to do was to know himself. With Sharon, he sometimes felt he was letting her down. She would disapprove, laugh at his ideas, criticise his clothes, take his hair-style or the lack of it as a personal insult. There was a tiredness about them. She loved him, surely. But the gaps between the moments of passion left him empty. They were not friends.

It was couples with Sharon. Boys and girls were couples. And if they were not already coupled, boys and girls went in search of this conventional bliss with the same zeal and hope (and desperation) that sustained Arthur's knights in their search for the Holy Grail. The great confidence trick, the great lie was the promise of salvation at the end of the rainbow. Disappointment, making do, being grown-up, facing up to reality, heterosexuality—the inevitability of it all, and the smugness of that inevitability offended the adventurer.

Now, after Matthew, waiting for Sharon, Phil was beginning to understand.

That evening Phil and Sharon talked. Instead of going to their usual pub, where they would have to share a table with people they knew, they caught a bus to Ealing and found a pub with a garden where they could be strangers and sit undisturbed.

He told her about his feelings for Matthew and she listened without wanting to understand. He didn't tell her about the afternoon, just that he and Matthew had spent it together. She didn't ask if anything happened. She didn't ask because she couldn't or didn't want to imagine what could have happened. If he'd spent the afternoon at home alone with a girl Sharon would have cross-examined him, almost hoping for an answer that would hurt. He explained about couples and settling for everyone else's idea of what was right and proper. He told her about the words on his locker door at school, and about Matthew's father and the attack outside the flats. He tried to explain about friends.

'We've all got friends,' she said. 'Anyway, you think too much.'

'Yeah. Maybe you're right.' At least he had tried. Sharon wasn't going to surprise him, he knew that much before he started. He hoped, however, for something more than a gentle put-down. She snuggled up to him.

'Do you love me?'

'I love you, Sharon,' he reassured her.

'That's nice,' she whispered. At that moment, with his arms around Sharon and her head pressed to his chest, Phil experienced a feeling of superiority. Quite simply, he knew more than she did. With that knowledge came an aloneness and their love became unequal.

We went for a walk then across Ealing Common towards the main road and the bus stop. We held hands, we cuddled, we did all the things lovers do in public places. Sharon was happy and, in a way, so was I.

When we got back to her house she asked me if I wanted to come in to say hello to her mum and dad. I told her I was tired and needed my bed. She was a bit disappointed but understood.

'See you tomorrow?' she asked.

'Sure.'

'Bye.'

'Bye.'

'Phil?' she called me back.

'What?'

'We're going to be alright, aren't we?'

'Yeah, course we are,' I said.

'Goodnight.' She blew me a kiss and waited by her door until I'd crossed the road and waved. She always did that, it was like a habit. It was things like that, the habits, that make couples out of people like us, I suppose.

When I got home, mum was watching the telly. I put my head round the door, said goodnight and went to the bathroom. Looking in the mirror I remembered Mr Cross's sexual orientation session.

'I wept for myself, but mostly I cried because I didn't conform,' Mr Cross read from his book.

''Cos he was a pervert, that's why.' Dennis always had the answers. 'There's twenty of us in here. . . Own up. Both of you. Who is it, then?'

'Anytime you need to talk, you know where to find me.' Mr Cross was baby-sitting that night.

'Well I think it's sad,' said Vi.

'Thank you, Vi.'

Phil didn't got to school the next morning, instead he went to the swimming pool where he knew he'd find Matthew .

The only other person there was an old man in a swimming cap, who was exercising in the section of the pool roped off from the diving area. Matthew was on the high-board preparing to dive.

'Matthew!' Phil's voice reverberated through the vast, tiled arena.

Matthew, caught at precisely the wrong moment, dropped his arms to his side. He saw Phil, a lonely match-stick figure in the stepped spectator area. 'Now what?' he snapped.

'We're off.' Phil called up to him. 'We're leaving, Matthew. We're going.'

Matthew laughed and pulled himself back into a diving position.

'Jump!' Phil shouted.

And he did. He sprang from the board, flew through the air and cut the water so cleanly there was hardly a ripple to mark his point of entry.

That afternoon, Phil and Matthew left London.

4

Seaford: A seaside resort in East Sussex, eight miles west of Eastbourne. Formerly at the mouth of the River Ouse, Seaford was a member of the Cinque Port of Hastings. In the sixteenth century the river changed course to Newhaven, three miles to the east, and Seaford declined as a port. It wasn't until the early nineteenth century that it found a measure of salvation in its new role as a watering-place.

A short climb to the stars from Seaford's wind-lashed sea front brings the day-tripper, or back-packer, or curious resident to Beachy Head, from where the hopeless may leap undisturbed; and to the Seven Sisters, those inscrutable, white-faced bitches, who stare out to sea like silent wreckers.

Conservatory-fronted hotels named after Spanish holidays, elder statesmen and Scottish pipe dreams line the front. Here, behind glass, bird-like old ladies and men with death creeping up their legs watch the wave-spray as it flies over the concrete sea breaks. They dare not promenade for fear of being de-permed, for fear of being exposed as stick-insects. For fear of being rolled by the wind.

Suzie, fifteen and already a vagrant, braved the wind and the spray as she walked towards the

Martello tower that guarded the east end of the front. Her hair was long and black and thick with sea salt, her clothes starched with dirt. She was probably pretty. Beyond the tower, a line of beach huts paraded in an orderly fashion.

Suzie had run away from home, a tarted-up Deptford terrace, eight weeks ago and chose, instead of the corniness of Piccadilly and its sad bedouins, to come to the coast with its memories of holidays, slot-machines, burgers and municipal rides.

Brighton jostled her back onto the road. Newhaven offered nothing but views of ferries heading out to sea. There's a doubtful glamour about those mini liners. She'd seen the adverts on television and knew all about the bars with their blazered barmen, and the restaurants, and the smiling crew retrieving lost teddy bears for grieving tots. Suzie had put away her teddy bears years ago, and hadn't the fare for a crossing. And so she came to Seaford, where there were no ferries. Here was a desert where she could be nothing more than a silhouette on the sea front.

Pete waited in Deptford. Had Suzie not run away, it would have probably all been over by now. Pete would have fondled Kate and Suzie would have danced with Steve. But she blew it. She ran away and broke poor Pete's heart. She did leave him a measure of fame, though. 'That's Suzie's boyfriend,' they'd say. He was warmly received at Suzie's home on his twice weekly visits. He would call round in case there was any news. He would be given tea, shown the photo albums and allowed to join in the family mourning. Once they even played a video for him of Suzie as a third year lion in her primary school's Christmas production of *The Wizard of Oz*.

He was committed, was Pete. To go out with anyone else now would be an act of betrayal so gross it didn't bear thinking about. Within two weeks of Suzie's disappearance, Pete's status was raised to that of childhood sweetheart. The girls in his class discovered aspects of his character, the way he looked, the clothes he wore that were suddenly and irresistibly attractive. The realised how sweet he was and how sad it all was. He was mothered and treated gently by all who came near him. They vied for his friendship. 'One day,' Pete thought darkly, 'I'll have an affair.' All he had to do was to choose: the lucky girl and the right moment. The rewards for Pete's constancy were manifold.

Romance.

It was night and we were still waiting for another lift. Matthew and I were carrying a sports bag each and we had a small tent, which he had tied to his bag. The tent belonged to Matthew's father, who used it for fishing. We'd borrowed it without his dad knowing.

The traffic raced past us. Too many horror

stories in the newspapers, I reckoned. They were all frightened that if they stopped they might pick up the latest rapist, or escaped nutter. 'Sun, sea, sand and romance,' I said. 'I like it.'

Matthew was getting pissed off with me by now. If I moaned it wasn't because I didn't want to be with him, of course I did, it was my idea. It was my idea to go in the first place.

'We're away, No more harassment,' he reminded me. Then it started to rain.

We had to leave when we did. If we'd planned it and thought it through and waited for the right time, one of us, probably me, would have bottled out. It wasn't that bad at home. Mum was alright and I'd kept myself to myself at school. I'd left the words on my locker door to show them all that I didn't care, and they more or less left me alone. They'd had their say, I suppose, and done their bit. But I had to get away before it got back to normal again; before it all got back to secrets and lies and Sharon telling me what Vera thought. It didn't matter if I missed school. I could have left last year if I'd wanted to. I'd only stayed on for the sixth form because I didn't much fancy any of the Youth Opportunities they were offering.

Matthew hadn't got a job to worry about, so he was alright. He hadn't really spoken to his parents since the thing with the magazines. He said it was like someone in the family had died and everyone was too embarrassed to talk about it. Home was just somewhere he slept.

We agreed to meet at my house in the afternoon before mum got back from work. I went round to see Todd, who worked in his brother's video shop, and told him what I was doing. He lent me fifty quid from the till and wished me luck. He knew about me and Matthew, or he guessed. We never talked about it, but I reckoned he must have known. When we were with Todd, or if we met him somewhere, he'd just take it that me and Matthew were together, like at the barbecue. I never heard him slag anyone off, or have a go about anything much. Todd just got on with his own life and went for it whenever he could, which was most evenings. If there was anything happening, if there was a good time to be had, he'd know about it and he'd be there.

'Send us a postcard,' he said.

'I will,' I promised. 'I'll make it a fruity one.'

I left a note for mum in the kitchen saying that I'd decided to have a sort of a holiday, which was true (or a holiday, which was sort of true), and telling her not to worry. I promised to phone her. If I moaned as we stood in the wet being sprayed by the lorries, it was because I hadn't thought it could take that long to get anywhere.

The rain got heavier and we'd given up hoping that anyone would stop for us when a car, a Ford Sierra, pulled up a few yards from where we were standing. Neither of us moved, we both just stood there staring at it. Maybe it hadn't stopped for us, maybe he'd just pulled over to look at a map or something. The driver sounded his horn.

'Come on,' Matthew yelled.

We both got into the back, thanked the bloke for stopping, and let the warmth get to us.

He was roughly middle-aged and a bit ponced-up with hair that looked like combed spaghetti. He told us he was a rep for a company which made harmonicas. 'Huge market. You'd be surprised,' he said. 'The people's musical instrument. Anyone can afford one. D'you play anything?'

'No,' we told him.

'Pity. Not even the piano? If you can play the piano, you can play anything.'

Matthew explained that he lived in a house that hadn't been designed for pianos. 'Never had a wall long enough for pianos', he said. 'What about you, Phil?'

'No,' I said. 'Never.'

'Pity. How far you going, then?'

'The seaside,' Matthew told him.

'That's nice, lads.' The driver beamed at us in his mirror. 'Holiday?'

'Honeymoon,' Matthew said, beginning to get cheeky. Any minute now, I thought, and we'd be back on the side of the road standing in the rain. I elbowed him hard in the ribs. The harmonica man laughed.

'Honeymoon? Quick workers, are you?'

'Speed of light, chief. That's us. Right, Phil?'

'Right,' I said.

'I could teach you lads a thing or two. You bet.'

'I bet,' Matthew said.

'They're a push-over. Promise them the moon and they'll settle for you.' He winked at me in his mirror. 'D'you know what I mean?'

'I bet you've had your share,' Matthew teased him. 'Go on. I bet you've had a few.'

'Had them all, mate,' he said. 'Big ones, small ones, black ones. They're exotic, the black ones, can't get enough of it. White ones. The lot.' He laughed. 'Honeymoon.'

'All girls, are they?' Matthew asked.

'What d'you mean?'

'Your collection, They're all women, are they?'

'I don't know what you mean.'

'We're with each other. It's our honeymoon,' Matthew told him.

The driver didn't say anything for a bit. I don't think he could work out whether Matthew was taking the piss or not. Maybe he had picked up a couple of nutters after all. Maybe he thought this was it, the ultimate big one: there were two of us and one of him. He kept chucking us quick looks in his mirror, checking out the danger that lurked on the back seat of his company Sierra.

'I don't know what you mean,' he repeated.

'Don't worry, mate.' I leant forward and whispered in the man's ear, 'You're not really our type.'

The car swung into the side of the road and climbed the verge, where it slid to a stop. Not many seconds later Matthew and Phil were back in the rain.

'Scum,' yelled the man who sold harmonicas. He had got them safely out of his car, and the nightmares that had been snaking through his mind a few moments ago had been seen off by a righteous rage. 'Perverts!' he screamed as the rain ran down his face. 'Animals. You're not even that. Filth! It's against the law!' Then, almost as an afterthought, 'It's against God's law!' He got back into his car, gunned the engine and span the wheels on the muddy verge.

'So's rape, mate!' Matthew shouted back. But the traveller was off, accelerating into the night towards yet another fantasy to add to his seedy collection.

'Now what?' Phil asked. It was, he reminded Matthew, mainly Matthew's doing that had lost them their ride.

'We wait for something a bit classier.'

'Rover, Jag, Datsun, Daimler,' Phil intoned as he watched the traffic speed past them. 'Bentley, XR, Beetle.'

'What are you doing?'

'Dreaming.'

They arrived in Seaford at dawn. The sea was high and the spray manic as it grabbed vainly at the sky. Phil and Matthew stood on the front by the

Martello tower watching a fishing boat steaming out into the waves. Tired beyond sleep and spiked on memories of home, they stared out to sea in silence. Seagulls wheeled overhead as though curious about the newcomers. A police car cruised slowly past. Curious or not it didn't stop.

'Sun, sand, sea and romance,' Matthew said, finally breaking the silence, 'Fuck it.'

Suzie slept on a deck-chair in Seeview, beach hut number thirty-three. She had wrapped herself in an old tablecloth, tea towels and a car-rug, and still the morning cold crept like damp, arthritic fingers along her body. She shivered in her sleep and pulled the car-rug tighter around her.

Matthew and Phil walked along the row of beach huts, trying each of the doors as they passed. The door to number thirty-three swung open and Suzie woke with a start.

'Sorry,' Matthew said. 'We thought it was empty.'

'Well it's not.' Suzie blinked against the dawn light and tried to make sense of the silhouettes in the doorway. 'Who are you?'

She looked a bit frightened. All she knew was that two blokes had broken into the hut. And it wasn't even her hut. Matthew explained that we were just looking for somewhere warm.

'So?'

'Well, that's it, really,' he said.

'Have you just got here?' Suzie asked.

'Yes,' I said. She sat up in her deck-chair and pulled the blanket up to her chin. I saw she was shivering.

'Shut the door,' she said. 'Where are you from?'

'London,' Matthew told her.

'Tourists?' she asked.

Now that she reckoned she wasn't going to get any hassle from us, the flashness was beginning to set in.

'Not exactly,' I said.

Matthew was sorting through the crap that was lying around the hut: a pile of old tea bags, a rusty kettle, a small gas cooker with an empty gas cylinder; a couple of mugs, the sort you get at petrol stations and a soggy copy of a gardening magazine.

'I've already done that,' Suzie told him. 'There's nothing here.'

A starfish had been nailed to the wall just above the door. Matthew reached out to touch it as though it were still alive.

'D'you live here?' he asked her.

'Hardly.' Then she smiled. 'I'm from London as well.'

'Tourist?' I asked her.

'Not exactly.' She laughed. 'D'you fancy a swim?'

Suzie shed her covers. She simply rose from the

deck-chair and let the covers fall to the floor. As she started to strip off the layers of clothing she wore to keep her bag light and the cold out, Matthew and Phil turned away.

'Don't worry,' she reassured them. She pulled off her T-shirt and dropped her trousers to reveal a one-piece swimming costume. 'See? Not even a bikini,' she said as she ran out of the hut.

Matthew and Phil rummaged through their bags for their swimming trunks and quickly changed. By the time they'd got down to the beach, Suzie was already in the cold, grey sea. She chose her waves carefully and let herself be carried, screaming and choking to the shallows.

Matthew and Phil watched her from the pebble beach.

'What d'you reckon?' Phil asked as Suzie grabbed another wave.

'I ain't getting wet.'

'About her. What d'you think?'

'She's alright.'

'Tasty?'

'Maybe.' Matthew lay back on the pebbles and shut his eyes.

'Pretty,' Phil said.

'Just that?'

'Just that.' He lay next to Matthew. 'What else?'

As the wave that carried her to the water's edge was sucked back out to sea, Suzie watched the boys. She wasn't sure yet. She thought they might be alright, but she wasn't sure, not yet. She needed time. All Suzie ever needed, or wanted, was time. She wanted time to think. Time to breathe and work things out. If only it could all be like a video, she thought. If only she could set the timer to record an emotion she hadn't time to deal with yet, or some important piece of life, an incident, a meeting, even a person. If she could set the timer to record it when she wasn't quite there, when she didn't have the time to be there, she could play it back later. She could rewind, pause, slow it down, fast forward it, erase it or snap the tab and keep it. If only she had the time. She hadn't even got round to God yet, no time. Or the ozone layer, acid rain, and whaling; or love and marriage, or sin, or learning to play a musical instrument. Even puberty was all a bit of a rush. Life's a bitch, she thought. And then you die.

Matthew and Phil raced towards her across the beach.

5

Sharon, on the other hand, had so much time she was drowning in it.

Phil and Matthew had been gone a day and a half (thirty-six hours that shook her world) and Sharon was already in deep mourning. There was no glamour in this adventure for her, though. Her boyfriend had run off with a poof, a queer, a nancy boy. The rejection was complete.

The story was that Phil was on an extended day-trip, but Vera knew the truth and pitied her. Vera pitying Sharon, there was the most painful of all humiliations. Sharon was the pretty one, the one with the pity. She looked good, she was admired by the boys and envied by the girls. Vera, on the other hand, was the clown, the joker, the fat girl with the square face and the home haircut. And Vera pitied Sharon. The injustice of it all offended beyond comprehension. She ached. She couldn't eat. Nothing held her attention for more than five minutes. She avoided mirrors; looking at her reflection only compounded the confusion. The pain she felt was physical, it left her dizzy and exhausted. Here, in Vera's bedroom, there was only one mirror and that was dusty and mottled and distorted enough not to matter.

All Sharon ever wanted was a steady boyfriend. She wanted someone to love and to make plans with. She wanted, more than anything, someone with whom she could wish away her adolescence. Time weighed heavy on Sharon.

'He'll phone,' she persuaded Vera. 'He'll phone. I know he'll phone.

'If he loves you.'

'He'll phone,' Sharon said.

'What if he don't?'

'Sod him, then.'

'Don't you care?'

'Of course I care, Vera. What do you think?'

'I don't know.' Vera settled in front of her mottled mirror and pulled at her hair. 'What about the AIDS?' she said.

'What about it?'

'It's a bleeding curse, that's what. Have you thought about it?'

'Of course I have,' Sharon had thought about it, she'd read about it, she'd even watched a programme all about it on television.

'It wouldn't have been so bad if he'd got run over, d'you know what I mean?' Vera was trying to be helpful. 'Or if he'd got done for something and got put away. You could visit him, then. couldn't you? But what happens if he comes back. . .'

'When he comes back,' Sharon snapped.

'What happens when he comes back? He might have caught it. Then what?' She asked.

'Shut-up, Vera.'

'Yeah. Okay. Sorry. It's a dog's bollocks, though, isn't it?'

'What is?'

'Life, Shazzer. It's about as useful to you and me as a dog's bollocks.

'I know what you mean,' Sharon sighed.

Vera came away from the mirror and went to the window. Twenty floors down was the courtyard around which the flats were built. What had once been a landscaped play area had become a windswept desert. She remembered standing at the same window ten years ago, when they first moved in and the flats where being renovated, watching the men from the council planting some trees. A week later the trees had disappeared. 'What do you want to do now?' she asked Sharon.

'Nothing. I don't want to do nothing.' Sharon was beginning to lose all patience with Vera. Vera couldn't begin to understand what she was going through. Nobody could. 'And don't call me Shazzer,' she said.

'Sorry.'

'If you must know, I'm going to go home and I'm going to sit by the phone. Okay?'

'Suit yourself.' Vera walked to the door and waited for Sharon to make a move. 'You going or what?' she asked, feigning indifference.

Sharon half rose, then fell back onto the bed and burst into tears. 'Oh, Vera. I feel such a prat.'

'Yeah, well.' Vera hurried over to Sharon and put her arms around her. As Sharon sobbed, Vera rocked her back and forth as she would a child.

Phil, Matthew and Suzie, wet and cold to the bone, ran back to the beach hut. An old weather-reddened couple watched them suspiciously from number thirty-nine's small verandah.

'Morning,' offered Matthew as he brazenly led the way into Seeview.

'How do,' said the couple from thirty-nine.

Once inside the hut, Matthew, Suzie and Phil quickly changed out of their swimming gear.

'We better get a move on,' Suzie said when she'd finished dressing. 'Before the neighbours get suspicious.'

She took them to a mini funfair next. It was a tawdry affair that sat like a giant, multi-coloured spider at the municipal, west end of the sea front. Here funsters could play the micro-chip arcades or race scaled down motor-bikes around a miniature circuit. For two ten pence coins the very young (or the very small) could straddle smiling dinosaurs and be made dizzy on creaking, slot-machine roundabouts; whilst those tall enough to see over the counters could buy dirty postcards, candy-floss, burgers, hot-dogs, and horoscopes in sealed envelopes.

At night, fairy lights sparkled over the rides and the stalls and around the entrance to the arcade. These lights, the electronic music from the games consoles and the steam rising from the burger and hot-dog stall, invested the ramshackle concession with something of the atmosphere of the real thing. In daylight, the funfair was as sad and as meaningless as the plastic eternity rings they sold next to the dirty postcards.

Suzie lifted a handful of toffees and a bar of chocolate from the sweet counter when the woman in charge was looking the other way.

'Supplements the dole,' she said. I was beginning to like Suzie.

'How long have you been here?' I asked her.

'Eight weeks.'

She moved on to Matthew, who was at the rifle-range in the arcade shooting ducks. I noticed a couple of girls sitting having tea in the cafeteria. They were tasty and one of them reminded me of Sharon. She didn't exactly look like Sharon, but she had the same colour hair and moved her hands like Sharon did when she spoke. They were brown with a foreign tan, and blond. One of them had her sunglasses pushed up into her hair, all a bit of a pose, really. Maybe they were foreign, in which case it would have been alright. I couldn't hear what they were saying or what language they were saying it in. I watched them until Matthew came over to me.

'Are you with us?' Him and Suzie had been watching me watch the girls.

'Just looking,' I said. 'I'll look at fellers if you'd rather.'

'What's he on about?' Suzie asked Matthew.

'Don't you know?' Matthew said. 'Haven't you guessed?'

'Guessed what?'

'We're with each other,' I said and grabbed Matthew's hand.

Suzie laughed. 'You're a couple of queers, then.' She looked at Matthew, then she looked at me, then she looked at Matthew again. 'Bloody hell,' she said. 'You're gay, aren't you?'

'Yes,' said Matthew.

'That's great. That's really great.' She looked at us both again as if something was bothering her. 'You don't look like queers.'

'Sorry,' I said.

'No. That's alright. That's really great.'

Just then three blokes walked up to the dirty postcard stand and started sorting through the racks. Suzie saw them and her mood changed. Suddenly she looked frightened.

'Let's go,' she said. 'I'm bored.'

The men saw her and one of them whistled. The other two laughed. Suzie grabbed our arms and tried to force us away.

'What's the hurry?' Matthew wanted to know.

'I told you, I'm bored.'

So we left the fair with Suzie in the middle holding on to our arms.

As we walked back to the centre of the town, I decided to phone home. Matthew wasn't too keen on the idea. He said I ought to be careful and to give it a day or two to let things cool down a bit. I didn't see why, though. All I wanted to do was to phone home and tell mum I was alright. If there was anything to cool down, a phone call was bound to help.

While Phil was making his call, Matthew and Suzie waited on the embankment of a play area that had been dug into a bowl to offer some protection against the wind. Tennis was played here and, at night, couples courted.

'Are you going steady, sort of?' Suzie asked Matthew.

'We're on our honeymoon.'

Suzie thought about this. She smiled. 'I like you, Matthew.'

'Yeah?'

'Yeah. You at school?'

'Left last year,' Matthew said.

'Got a job?'

'What do you think?'

'We're two of a kind, mate,' she said. 'Outlaws.'

'Freedom.' He got up and ran to the centre of the bowl. 'Freedom!' he shouted.

Suzie ran across to him and he caught her in his

arms and swung her round. Phil saw all this from the phone box. He couldn't hear what they were saying, but he saw them hug. They looked happy and he felt excluded. Matthew didn't want him to phone home and now he was hugging Suzie. He said goodbye and hung up as Matthew turned to him, waved his arms and shouted something. Whatever it was he said was carried away by the wind long before it could reach Phil. It was in fact 'Freedom!', a shout of joy he wanted to share.

6

That night they pitched their tent high on a rise within sight of the Seven Sisters. They'd left Suzie outside a pub in the centre of the town.

'I could show you around,' she had offered. 'I know all the scams.'

Phil wasn't keen on taking Suzie along with them.

'You want to be alone, right?' Suzie asked, reading Phil's mood.

'We'll meet up later,' Matthew promised her.

'That's okay.' Suzie shrugged. 'Because I've got things to do, anyway. People can be really strange round here. Maybe you'll get in the way, d'you know what I mean?'

She watched them walk off in the direction of the sea. She waited, hoping for a backward glance, a change of heart, maybe. She liked Matthew and Phil. They were different. They were wrapped up in each other enough not to be bothered by the fact that she was a girl. It didn't matter to them whether she was attractive or not and that freed her in a way that was new and exciting. She'd almost forgotten the way she looked. Glances in shop windows weren't enough to remind her. There was bound to be a mirror somewhere in the pub, she thought, probably in the ladies. She'd go in, she'd buy a half if she had to, and she'd find the mirror. Tomorrow, she'd look for them again. Once Matthew and Phil were out of sight, Suzie pushed open the pub door and walked into the smoke-thick, neon-lit bar.

The spot they chose was windswept and loud with the sound of the waves. The sea shimmered with reflected moonlight and the cliff faces shone as though lit from below. Here was a wild place, a place so utterly self-possessed it offered neither threat nor comfort.

'Freedom,' Matthew said once they had settled in their sleeping bags and wriggled and beaten some kind of comfort out of the rough grass beneath the ground-sheet. 'How do you reckon Suzie's getting on?'

'Do you wish she was here?' Phil asked.

'No.'

'I saw you snogging with her.'

'We weren't snogging, we were cuddling.'

'You were cuddling,' Phil said. 'She was snogging.' He turned to lie on his back and stared up at the light from the small torch that hung from the ridge pole. 'She fancies you.'

'Phil?'

'What?'

Their voices were dulled and flattened by the acoustics of the tent.

'I'm here, aren't I? We're here together. Just us.'

'Yeah. Just us.'

This was the first time they had been so completely alone. They listened to the sound of the wind drumming against the tent and, beyond that, the roar of the sea. Nobody was going to surprise them.

'What did your mum have to say?'

'Not a lot,' Phil said. 'Sharon's been round.'

'And?'

'She reckons you're a bad influence. As it happens, I don't care.' He turned back to Matthew. 'Have you ever. . .'

'What?'

'You know.'

'I don't.'

'Have you ever been with someone,' Phil whispered as though *someone* might overhear.

'Once,' Matthew said. 'He wanted sex. I wanted romance.' He laughed softly. 'Sounds daft, doesn't it?'

'No.'

'Was it the queer feller from the bar?'

'No. What about you and Sharon?'

'Of course we have.'

'Good?'

'Brilliant,' he lied. The few times he had done it with Sharon it was rushed when it should have been tender; and dangerous when it should have been easy. 'But I'm here, with you,' Phil said.

Matthew unzipped his sleeping bag. Phil leant across and kissed him on the lips. 'I love you,' he said, then he kissed him again.

Matthew reached up and pulled Phil's head down onto his chest. 'It's alright,' he whispered. 'It's alright.'

'I know it's alright.'

Phil eased out of his sleeping bag and slid in next to Matthew. They held on to each other. Neither dared move, or say anything more. They simply held on to each other. There was no rush now. No need to be furtive. There would be no graffiti on locker doors, or chants in the changing room at the swimming pool. There was no Sharon, or Vera, or stone-throwing to avoid. Dennis the Greek and all the mindless cruelty he carried around with him (like a thug carries a flick-knife) was safely tucked up in the world they'd left behind for a while.

I held on to Matthew long after he'd gone to sleep. I just lay there without moving. I breathed as quietly as I could. I wanted to hear him breathe and feel him move against me. I did love him, especially then. I'd never spent the night with anyone before, not even with Sharon. And here I was with Matthew. Here I was with a bloke.

I remembered the first time we met. He'd come from another school across London when his parents moved. I liked him then, and I admired him. I liked the way he looked and how in control he was. That was the big thing with Matthew, control. There was nothing flash about him, he just knew how to handle himself. He never had a girlfriend, but then a lot didn't and that didn't mean anything. When we started going swimming together it was his idea. He was a diver, he told me. He was always a bit frightened of the high-board, but he said that was a good thing. It kept it safe and helped him to concentrate.

It wasn't until he'd left school that I realised how much I really did like him. I missed him in the classroom. I missed getting to school and seeing him there. We started meeting in the evenings. Instead of just meeting by accident, we'd arrange it. It was like a date when it was just the two of us. I'd look forward to it for days. Sometimes he'd come round to my house, or I'd visit him. Sometimes we'd all go out together, him, me and Sharon. She soon got pissed off with it, though, and said that she wouldn't mind it so much if he brought a girl along with him so we could be a foursome. But Matthew never had a girlfriend. We spent more and more time on our own. It got so that I'd not go out with Sharon to be with him. There was nothing going on or anything, but the more I saw of him, the closer I wanted to be to him. I even got jealous of his other friends.

Sometimes I'd not see him for a week. He'd go up to the West End every evening for a week. If I asked why, or what he did when he got there,

'You know, this and that,' he'd say, 'Just looking around.' So I didn't ask anymore. Once, though, I did say it would be fun if we could go together. He wasn't too keen and I never said it again.

He told me later that he had a friend who was a busker at the Tottenham Court Road Underground. He was a bloke called Roger, who he had a thing with. Nothing happened, he said. They just really liked each other and Matthew would help him out with getting the money. Afterwards, when it was time to give up the pitch, or when the law moved them on, they'd go to a club, a gay club, where they were known and liked and were not bothered by anyone.

I'd never been to one of those places. I thought they would be full of men dressed as women talking with lisps and calling each other by girl's names. 'Too much television,' he told me. 'You're buying their bullshit.'

I woke him up by kissing him on the neck and on the lips. I kissed his arms and his shoulders. Even though he was lying there next to me, I suddenly missed him. I remembered the barbecue and how much I wanted to be with him then. It was all fun, and new. I wanted Matthew to wake up before the morning. I never felt like that about Sharon, but then I'd never spent a whole night with her.

'Matthew,' I whispered.

'What?'

'I love you.'

He forced himself awake and put his hands to my face. He held me like that for a long time and just looked at me. If Sharon had ever looked at me like that, I would have been embarrassed. Maybe that's because I knew her too well.

Then we slept.

Romance.

7

The next morning, Police Constable Paul Leesley of the East Sussex Constabulary was on the early shift. His first duty of the day was to clear away any human debris that might offend the townspeople of Seaford when they woke. Everything should be as it was left the night before. People who paid their rates expected that their streets, their town, would be kept clear of the unexpected.

When a man wished to take an early morning stroll along the sea front, or across a park, or to the corner shop, he wished also to establish that there had been no fundamental changes to his world overnight. The stroll would be a confirmation of his inalienable right to constancy.

That morning, as on the previous four mornings, it fell on Police Constable Leesley to uphold this inalienable right. One of Leesley's particular obsessions was campers—'pirate campers', he called them. This scruffy, unwashed, group of free-loaders, who refused to use the facilities offered by the official camp-sites, were visited on him, he was convinced, by an angry god, against whom he had dared to sin. Unknowingly, he must have at least once deeply offended a deity with a sadistic sense of retribution. To the constable, campers, backpackers and vagrants were all simply 'fuckin' hippies', scum who littered the landscape and corrupted everything they came in contact with.

He listened to Pink Floyd and Chris De Burgh and once went to a Moody Blues concert at Wembley. He used to like Joan Armatrading, but stopped listening to her records when he heard that she lived with another woman. He felt a massive sense of betrayal when he heard about Joan Armatrading. Hers were the albums he never replaced on C.D.

He had three children, to whom he was a good father, and he had never been seriously unfaithful to his wife. He was forty-three years old and hadn't yet sat the sergeant's exam. With promotion come responsibilities, with responsibilities come desks and with desks comes paperwork. He'd seen too many good coppers buckle under the weight of a sergeant's stripes. He was quite happy, thank you very much, being out and about on patrol in his Rover three-point-five. Constable Leesley was his own man. True he was radio-linked to the shop, but he did enjoy a measure of freedom and he was not about to let promotion interfere with any of it.

He knew all about Suzie, he'd seen her around the town but had never managed to corner her. She was harmless, just another runaway, easy meat. He'd have her when he was good and ready. She'd be a present for the social services when he got round to wrapping her up.

Police Constable Leesley swung the car off the station forecourt and headed through the empty streets towards the Martello tower and the beach huts. He remembered seeing two boys, youths with sports bags, hanging around the tower a couple of mornings ago. They looked harmless enough and he hadn't seen them since.

He cruised past the beach huts and along the track that eventually led to the cliff tops. This is where the 'pirate campers' came. Sure enough, a tent had been pitched some hundred yards off the track in a hollow just below the cliff top. Constable Leesley stopped his car and turned off the engine. His radio, it was loud and intrusive in the morning stillness, crackled.

Leesley contemplated the tent through his windscreen. He could drive up to within inches of it and sound his horn; or he could switch on his siren, that screaming din that raced the adrenalin through his body; that would shake them. Or he could simply rip the tent out of the ground. There wouldn't be any complaints, he'd see to that, and if there were, they would fall on deaf ears. He started up the car and rolled towards the tent. He drove to within five feet from it and braked. Then he remembered that today was his eldest son's fifteenth birthday and he lost all interest in violence. He would just tell them to move on. He didn't need the hassle, not today. Today he would be generous in honour of his eldest son.

He got out of the car and walked to the tent. He unzipped the entrance flap and shoved his head in through the gap. The sight that confronted him was so offensive, so disgusting, so unnatural it turned his stomach. He could feel the puke rising to his throat. Matthew and Phil were in each others arms, asleep in the same sleeping bag.

'Out!' he bellowed. 'Out!' He stepped back from the tent and took a deep breath to fight the nausea and to steady himself. 'Out!'

Phil pulled the tent flap back and blinked against the morning light. The constable swam slowly into focus.

'You!' Leesley yelled. 'You and your bit of stuff. Out!'

Phil quickly ducked back inside and shook Matthew awake. 'It's the Law. Get dressed,' he said.

Matthew snapped into consciousness. 'We were keeping warm, right?' he said.

Leesley walked back to his car and waited. The radio crackled out its messages of petty crime and local gossip, but Leesley's attention was focused firmly on the tent.

When Matthew and Phil finally did emerge, Leesley yelled at them to take the tent down.

The sound of the waves and the roar of the wind was alien and threatening, when last night it had been wild and perfect.

When we'd packed our stuff and put the tent away, the copper got out of his car and came towards us.

'I've got no time for you and your kind,' he said. 'No time.'

All we could do was to stand there. He walked back to his car, then he stopped and turned to us again.

'No time,' he repeated. It was as though we had made him sad. He wasn't yelling anymore. 'Just get your things and go,' he said. 'Go home. Go back to where you came from.'

He went back to his car, got in and drove off. We waited until the car was out of sight, then Matthew and me walked to the track and followed it down to the front. Neither of us said anything. We were both embarrassed at being caught by the copper.

Suzie spotted us as we came towards the beach huts.

'Oi!'

Matthew saw her first.

'Shit,' I said. I didn't feel like Suzie, not just now.

She was running towards us from the beach. We waited for her to catch up. I wanted to pretend we hadn't seen her and keep going, but Matthew waited.

'We're off,' I told her.

'Where to?' she asked.

'We don't know,' Matthew said. 'Anywhere.'

'Don't you like it here, then?'

'We thought we'd try somewhere else,' I

explained. 'We never planned to stay anywhere long anyway. Keep moving, that's us. Right, Matthew?'

'We were caught kipping together,' Matthew said. 'The Law caught us sleeping together.'

'Keeping warm,' I reminded him. 'We were keeping warm, right?' I carried on walking then.

'I prefer sleeping together. Don't you?' I heard Suzie say. 'It's warmer.'

Matthew let her come with us. He told me later that he felt sorry for her. Suzie reckoned that if we'd follow the beach round towards Newhaven, we would be alright. The Law kept away from there because there were no tracks, it was just rocks and cliffs; and small, pebbled beaches when the tide was out.

They walked in single file along the front. Phil led the way, Matthew followed him and Suzie brought up the rear.

'I don't know what I'm doing with you lot,' she shouted above the noise of the wind, which whipped in off the sea.

'You picked us up,' Phil yelled.

'You like us,' said Matthew.

'We're alright,' Phil said.

Each concentrated on walking in a more or less straight line. It was easier to deal with the wind and the spray in single file; each responsible only for themselves.

'We're wonderful!' Matthew sang. The wind and the sea and Suzie's apparently indomitable spirit had cheered them up. And they had got away with it. They'd been let off. They hadn't been arrested or asked any questions. They were free again.

'You're learning about life,' Phil shouted.

'Fair enough,' said Suzie.

On a sea-break that crossed the beach, dissecting it from the front to the sea, were the three men from the mini-funfair. They posed in water shorts and sawn-off sweat-shirts for the benefit of two women. They were ostensibly exercising around a rusty bar that had been set in the concrete for a purpose long forgotten. The women, who, unlike the men, were well wrapped against the cold, drank lager from cans. They were all drunk and bored and waiting for the night. In the meantime they would sit there on the cold concrete and make the smallest of small talk. Whatever shallows their minds sunk to, whatever small deaths they planned or relived, whatever their guilt, their love of the sea and the sounds and the smell of it would always redeem them.

One of the men spotted Suzie. 'Jailbait!' he called.

The women looked over and laughed. They held up their cans of lager in a mock salute.

'Suzie!' another of the men howled. 'Sooooozie!'

'Let's go,' Suzie said. She ran across the road into a builder's wasteland.

'What's all that about?' Phil asked when they caught up with her.

'Nothing. I just don't want to see them.'

'See who?' Phil shouted, out of breath and irritated by the mystery.

'Those blokes.' Suzie said. 'Those prats on the beach.'

'Who are they?' Matthew asked.

'Trouble.'

I was ready to junk her. This was all supposed to be about me and Matthew. It was our time, and Suzie was hijacking it. I didn't care anymore that she made us laugh.

'What sort of trouble?' I asked her.

'Trouble,' she said. 'Just trouble.'

We followed her for about half an hour along the beach to a place she said nobody ever used. We had to climb rocks and jump over pools of water that had been left behind by the tide to get there.

'There. What did I tell you?' Suzie stood on a rock and held her arms out as though she wanted us to cheer. She was right, though. It was private and it was cut off. Matthew clapped and Suzie bowed.

There was an old gun tower, which looked as if it was growing out of the rocks like a concrete tree with no leaves. We climbed up into it and looked out to sea through the slit they'd made for the gun. I didn't fancy it for long. It smelled of shit, human shit, I thought. I found a used condom on the floor and kicked it towards Suzie. 'I thought you said no one ever came here,' I said.

'No one except me.' She laughed and climbed back down to the rocks.

Later, when we'd got the tent up, the three of us sat down by the water's edge. I asked her again about the blokes on the beach.

'I met them when I first came here,' she told us. 'They were friendly faces, I thought. I thought they were what I needed. They knew what it was all about.'

'Like you do.' I said.

'No, not like me.' She was pissed off with that. 'I haven't tried to screw you, have I?'

'And they did?' Matthew asked.

'Yes. And they did.'

'They raped you?'

'Not exactly,' she said. 'I told you, they were friendly faces.'

'Then what?' I asked her.

'I tried to keep out of their way. I told them I was under age. But they still hassled me.'

'Just tell them to lay off,' I told her.

'They're blokes and I'm a female vagrant.'

'I'll tell them, then,' Matthew offered.

'And when you've finished with them,' said Suzie, 'I'll give you the rest of my hit-list.'

I picked up a stone and threw it out to sea. There wasn't a lot we could say, really. Matthew got up and stripped, right there, right in front of her. She watched him as he ran into the sea.

'I've got a feller back home,' Suzie told me. 'Well, I did have. He's probably given me up by now.'

[But he hadn't. Nor had Pete had his affair yet.]

'When are you going back?' I asked her.

'I'm not.'

She got up and, like Matthew, she took off all her clothes. Suzie was beautiful, that's a fact. She didn't mind me looking at her. Seeing her standing there, naked, I thought about her feller. Did he miss her? It was strange seeing her without her clothes on. I knew Suzie as a runaway, which is what she was and what she looked like in her dirty jeans and pullovers and torn jacket. Now, with nothing on, she looked normal. She looked like she lived up the road and had just come down to the beach for a giggle with her mates.

'You coming in?' she asked me.

I wanted to touch her. It wasn't a horny feeling. Just to feel her skin would have been nice. I felt sorry for her, that was it. Seeing her standing there, I felt sorry for her; I felt sort of sad for all of us.

'No,' I said.

She ran into the sea and jumped on Matthew. I didn't mind.

8

That night the three of them shared the tent. Matthew and Phil were already in their sleeping bags when Suzie crawled in from the beach. She was wearing just a T-shirt and a pair of knickers. She'd washed all her other clothes in the sea and had spread them over the rocks to dry.

'Okay, guys,' she said wriggling in between the two boys. 'I sleep in the middle, and no funny business. Know what I mean?'

'What's going on?' Phil asked.

'We're all mates.' she explained.

'Right,' said Phil.

'But it's our honeymoon,' Matthew protested as he made room for Suzie. 'That's what we're here for—funny business.'

'Self control, boys. Anyway, I might get jealous.'

'Do I get a kiss?' Phil wanted to know.

'Who from?' asked Suzie.

'I don't mind.'

'Tart,' Matthew said.

'Scrubber,' added Suzie. Then she kissed Phil on the cheek.

In London that night, Sharon and Vera went to the disco. It was the usual venue, the back room of the Spread Eagle. The queer feller from the bar was there with a friend. All the other couples were there too: people Phil and Sharon knew, mates from school. They were all there.

At first Sharon didn't want to go in. She had spent all afternoon round at Vera's making-up and trying on a variety of skirt and top combinations, which she had brought in a suitcase.

'Leaving home?' her father had asked as she left the house.

'That's not funny,' Sharon replied. She slammed the street door so hard the living-room windows rattled.

Hours later and she'd lost her nerve. They stood outside the pub shivering in the night chill.

'Come on,' pleaded Vera. 'You persuaded me to come, remember? It was you who wanted to come.'

'I've changed my mind. Let's go somewhere else.'

'Not now that we're here. Come on, Sharon.'

'I can't, Vera. I can't go in there.'

'Of course you can. They'll be queuing up to dance with you. You look great.'

'I don't care about that.'

'Yes you do,' Vera said. 'You care, Sharon. That's why you wanted me to come with you, isn't it?'

'What are you on about?'

'You know what I mean. Look at me. Look at

you. Don't I make you look good? Now come on, before you really get on my tits.' She was beginning to lose patience with Sharon. 'Stop pissing around. Because if you don't get your finger out and start putting it about a bit, I'll do it for you.'

'You don't like discos.'

'I do now.'

Vera walked into the pub and crossed to the back room. Sharon was left with no option but to follow. Returning home early and alone on a Saturday night was unthinkable. Vera, her friend (her fat friend, her side-kick, the moon to her sun) had left her with no option.

In the disco, the music was loud and crushing. Couples jostled for position on the dance floor. Sharon followed Vera through the mêlée to the make-shift bar, where the singles hung out. The queer feller spotted her and smiled.

'There you go,' said Vera. 'He fancies you.'

'Thanks. That's all I need,' Sharon hated it. She hated being there. She hated Vera. She especially hated the queer feller from the bar. 'Fuck off,' she mouthed at him. The queer feller jerked his head towards his friend. 'Chance would be a fine thing,' he mouthed back.

Dennis the Greek sidled over. 'Hello, girls,' he slurred drunkenly, though he wasn't even remotely drunk. Dennis had only ever been drunk once. It was in Bayswater at his cousin's wedding. His father thrashed him when they got home, not for being drunk, he explained, but for puking over the back seat of the new Carlton. He was thrashed for not being man enough to hold his liquor. Since then Dennis only ever drank shandy. He'd worked on his drunken act and perfected it in the hope that, coupled with his almost moustache, it would make him more attractive to the women, as he preferred to call them. The women, for their part, thought Dennis a prat. In time, these rejections would turn Dennis into a true alcoholic.

'Hello, Dennis,' said Sharon. 'Meet Vera.'

'Hi, Vera.' Dennis offered his hand. As Vera took it, he rolled almost imperceptibly on the balls of his feet. Oh, it was a good act. Nothing too extreme or too sudden. It was all quite subtle and very convincing.

'Is he drunk?' Vera asked Sharon.

'No.'

'Course I'm not.' He downed the remainder of his half a shandy in one and burped. 'Phil still away, is he?'

'Yes, Phil's still away. And so is Matthew. Anything else you need to know?'

'No. Just thought about how you were fixed, that's all.'

'That's nice of you, Dennis. Nice of you to ask.'

'I like you, Sharon. You're alright.' He meant it, and Sharon knew he did.

'Thanks,' she said. 'Thanks, Dennis.'

'Have you got a fag?' he asked to cover his embarrassment.

'Don't smoke,' Sharon said. 'But I'll dance with you if you like.'

'Really? You'll dance with me?' Dennis couldn't believe his luck. And it was to be so public. He'd be seen dancing with Sharon, with Phil's girlfriend. A thought suddenly struck him. A cruel, bastard of a blow. 'I can't dance,' he blurted.

'Never mind,' Vera said, quick as a flash. 'I'll teach you.' She took the empty glass from his hand and gave it to Sharon. Then, before either Dennis or Sharon could protest, she grabbed poor Dennis by his sleeve and pulled him towards the centre of the dance floor.

'You're a Greek, aren't you?' said Vera.

'Yes. My parents are from Cyprus.'

'Well I'm a gipsy. And I can see into the future.'

'Really?'

'It's your lucky night, sunshine.'

Sharon watched them dance. Dance after dance after dance. Nobody asked her to dance. Nobody tried to chat her up or even buy her a drink. She was still Phil's girlfriend. She missed him, especially now. People came over to talk, to ask her if she'd heard from him.

'How's Phil, then?'

'Heard from Phil, have you?'

'You alright, are you?'

'Has he sent you a card yet?'

'I wouldn't let mine piss off like that, no chance.'

'You missing him, are you?'

'I like your hair.'

Nobody mentioned Matthew. She wanted so much to hate Phil. How she missed him.

The queer feller from the bar, however, didn't miss a trick. One day, he really would write it all down. He caught Sharon's eye. This time she smiled. He winked. She shrugged and they ignored each other for the rest of the night.

9

The next morning, Sharon woke still thinking of Phil. When she'd got in after the disco, her mother told her that someone had called late from a phone box but couldn't get through. It could have been Phil. Sharon's mum was sure it was Phil, and so was Sharon. But it wasn't Phil. It was just kids messing about in the phone box on the corner. They weren't to know what emotions, hopes, expectations their mindless little game would set in motion.

Dennis stared across the breakfast table at the phone. His sister, who was a year older than him and dressed for church, watched him over the rim of her coffee cup.

'Are you expecting someone to ring you?' she asked.

'No.'

'Then why are you staring at the phone?'

'I'm not staring at the phone. If you must know, I'm thinking.'

'Dad says that I can go with you next week if you promise to get me back home by ten,' she announced.

'Piss off,' said Dennis.

Todd woke with an ache. He hadn't closed his brother's video shop until eleven-thirty, it being Saturday night and soft porn being the drunks' favourite accompaniment to the chinese take-away. She had come in again, the black girl with the Scottish accent, who took out Fatal Attraction every Saturday night. She'd been coming into the shop for the past four months and they always kept a copy of the video for her. Last night, for the first time, she was happy to chat. She was living on her own, she said, and Fatal Attraction reminded her why. Most Saturday nights someone tried to pick her up. More often than not she was tempted to take a chance. Instead, she'd take out Fatal Attraction.

Todd saw his chance and told her that there had been a mix-up and that the last copy of the video, the copy he'd meant to save for her, had been booked out earlier that evening. He was sorry for the inconvenience and offered to buy her dinner.

'Okay,' she said.

So Todd woke with an ache. What if he never saw her again?

The queer feller from the bar didn't get home that night. He and his friend left the disco half an hour before closing time and caught a cab to the Embankment, from where they were going to walk to

Battersea, where his friend shared a flat. They got jumped by six booze-blind thugs, who'd missed the last train to Cambridge. Their crime was to be seen holding hands on Vauxhall Bridge. The police were sympathetic but philosophical.

Pete woke early and was out of the house by eight. He'd arranged to go to church with Elizabeth, a pretty but prematurely frumpy cousin of Suzie's. They were to pray for Suzie's safe return. Pete and Suzie's cousin were in love and used prayer as a cover for the affair they both dreamed of.

Vera stayed in bed until midday. She thought about Dennis and remembered that they'd promised to phone each other. She wasn't that sure that she wanted to talk to him, not yet. She needed to think.

Romance.

Suzie was up and out of the tent long before either Matthew or Phil woke. She checked on her clothes, which were still wet. She'd wait for the sun. It was bound to come. The sun would do the trick. The sea was as still and as flat as she'd ever seen it. She looked up at the sky. It was grey and cloudy and heavy with the residue of a night mist. Today, thought Suzie as she watched the seagulls patrol their air space from their cliff-face nests, today would be a good day.

Matthew picked his way towards her across the

rocks. Beyond him, she saw Phil emerge from the tent and climb to the gun tower. They were all still together. They could stay here in their rocky kingdom forever if they chose to. Here could be defended against all comers. They had the cliffs behind them, the sea ahead of them and a tortuous journey over boulders and tide pools to their flanks. It was going to be a good day. She waved.

Matthew settled on a large rock. 'We need to talk,' he said.

'We could stay here forever.' Suzie said. 'FOR-EVER!' she shouted.

Matthew picked up a stone and threw it at the sea.

From his position at the centre of the tower floor, the shape and the curve of the gun slit gave a cinemascopic frame to Phil's view. Matthew and Suzie, placed as they were amongst the rocks at the foot of the cliff, were like characters in a sweeping epic.

'We both really like you,' Matthew told Suzie. He was uneasy and Suzie sensed it.

'And I like you, both of you. So that's alright, then, isn't it?' she said. 'Maybe we will stay here forever.' Matthew threw another stone at the sea. 'We planned to be alone,' he finally said.

'Right.'

'D'you understand?'

'Of course I understand,' Suzie said. Matthew smiled at her. It wasn't going to be too difficult after all, he thought. 'I understand I'm getting in the way,' she continued.

'It's not like that.' Matthew felt cheated.

'What is it like then?' Suzie was grabbed by an irrational fear. They wanted to get rid of her. The fear gave way to anger. The bastards didn't want her hanging around any more. Her instinct was to hit Matthew; to smash his face, now the face of a stranger, to a pulp.

'I'm gay.'

'I know that.' She tried to sound bored.

'And I'm with Phil,' he continued. 'We both get a lot of stick back home.'

'We all do.'

'Which is why we're here. We just want to get on with it.'

'I'm hardly stopping you, am I?'

'You are,' he said.

If he wanted her to go, then he would have to tell her. He'd have to say it. Suzie was not about to make anything any easier for anyone. It didn't help that they liked her. Enough people liked her in Deptford, and that didn't help. 'So you want me to piss off, do you?'

'I don't know.'

'Don't lie, Matthew,' she snapped.

Matthew searched for another stone. As Suzie watched him fumbling at the ground, she tried to hate him.

Matthew looked up at her. 'I'm sorry,' he said.

I could see what was going on down below me on the rocks. I couldn't hear what they were saying to each other, but I knew that Matthew was going to try to get Suzie to leave. We'd talked about it when we woke up and found ourselves alone in the tent, and we both agreed that Suzie had to go.

I saw her grab Matthew's hands and make him touch her tits.

'You can touch me, if you like,' she said.

Matthew pulled his hands away from her. 'Come on, Suzie.'

'Why not?'

'You know why not.'

Suzie smiled. 'There you are,' she said. 'You see? We're just people.'

'Mates,' Matthew agreed.

'Mates. Just mates.'

The wind came up without warning, hissing in across the sea and booming onto the cliff wall. The seagulls screamed as Suzie scrambled across the rocks to retrieve a sock that was flapping along the ground like an injured bird. 'Nearly dry,' she shouted, waving the sock above her head.

Matthew (and Phil from his tower) watched as Suzie leapt from rock to rock gathering up the rest of her clothes before the wind scattered them. She returned to Matthew with her clothes safely bundled in her arms and sat next to him.

'If you were here with your bloke. . .' he started.

'I haven't got a bloke.'

'The one who's given up waiting, then. If you were here with him, if you could be together, just the two of you, you'd want it, wouldn't you?'

'Yes. Maybe,' she said softly. 'And I thought it was going to be a good day today.' She sighed. Today she felt like wearing clean clothes for the first time in weeks. 'I wanted to look nice.'

'You do look nice.'

She pulled her knees up to her chin. 'Thanks,' she said.

'If you could have the time, you'd want it.'

'What about friends?'

'Phil and me are lovers. We do it. We sleep together. We kiss. We hold hands. We touch, same as the other lot, your lot, trying it on in discos and dark corners. D'you want me to go on?'

Suzie shrugged. 'Why choose, anyway?' she said. 'Same, opposite, both sexes. Whatever. Hetero, Bi, Homo, it's all labels. Designer sex. We're all mixed up, mate. We're all part of the same con. Do you reckon you could never do it with a girl?'

'I didn't say that,' Matthew replied.

'What, then?'

'I'm happy as I am.'

'You're chicken.'

'Hardly,' he said

'So you want me to go?'

'Yes.'

'When?'

'Today.'

They sat there for long time. I don't think they said too much. When Suzie got up and went to the tent, Matthew walked down to the sea and tried to skim some stones across the water, but it was getting rough and he didn't have much luck. I wanted to be with him, but I thought it might be better to keep out of the way. I thought as I was watching him there, alone on the beach, that I still didn't really know Matthew that well. Maybe he did want me to go down to him. Maybe he was happier on his own.

Another thing Phil, Matthew and Suzie did not know was that Police Constable Leesley had matched Suzie's description with that of a Susan Burton, aged fifteen, who had disappeared from her school in Deptford eight weeks ago. She had missed French on a Thursday afternoon and was never seen again.

Constable Leesley was prompted to check through the files (the paperwork he so loathed) when the landlord of a pub in Seaford's town centre informed him that a raggedly dressed and unhygienic young girl had spent an unusually long time in the ladies' toilet two evenings ago. The landlord suspected drug abuse. Leesley suspected the truth.

Matthew and Phil had agreed to walk Suzie back to Seaford. There, they could get something to eat and, maybe, go to the mini funfair and shoot some more ducks.

'You will come back here, though, won't you?' Suzie asked.

'Sure,' said Matthew.

'Promise?'

They promised her they would come back if they could.

'It's the best place in the world,' she said.

A storm was building as they took down their tent. The wind was gusting strongly now and the sea was beginning to sound out the rocks.

They walked to Seaford in silence, preoccupied with their own thoughts. The closer they got to the town the more each of them wanted to say: Phil wanted to explain; Matthew wanted to apologise; Suzie wanted to say that she understood, that she still thought of them as friends, nice people, that she was glad she met them. She wanted to wish them good luck, lots of love, happy endings, etc., etc., etc.

Police Constable Leesley and WPC Fletcher watched the Martello Tower and the approach to the beach huts from the shadow of the Hibernian hotel. As Suzie, Matthew and Phil came into view, Leesley shoved the Rover into gear. He waited for his chance.

'That's her,' he said, indicating Suzie through the windscreen.

'Sodding go, then,' WPC Fletcher barked.

Leesley knew that a hasty move would make Suzie break and run down to the beach, where they could easily lose her. He saw that she was about to cross the road. 'We'll have her,' he purred. That was when she would be at her most vulnerable. Childhood conditioning insisted that crossing a road was a journey of extreme peril. All the senses, therefore, would be concentrated on that one act. 'If you want to catch a thief,' Leesley told Fletcher. 'Catch him when he's crossing the road.'

Within seconds of Suzie stepping off the kerb, the police Rover had skidded to a halt at her feet. Leesley and Fletcher leapt out of the car, grabbed Suzie and bundled her into the back. Suzie clawed at the rear window, her eyes fixed on Matthew and Phil, who could do nothing but stand and watch until the car had turned out of sight.

'What was all that about?' Phil was rooted to the spot by the speed of the attack.

Matthew had already started to walk away. 'It's got nothing to do with us,' he shouted back at Phil. 'We're not meant to be here. Remember?'

'We can't just leave her,' Phil protested.

'Don't get involved. That's the rule.'

'Who's rule?'

'Their rule. It's called keeping out of trouble.'

'It's called bottling out.'

'Please yourself,' Matthew said.

'But we ain't done nothing!' Phil yelled at him. He yelled at the wind, at the sea, at anyone who cared to listen. Matthew had already put twenty yards between them.

10

They did go back to Suzie's beach that day. The storm was at its height when they returned, but there was a warmth in the familiarity of the rocks, and the wind and the spray was like a wall that only they could penetrate. They sat close to each other, their feet in the rain, under a small overhang at the foot of the cliffs.

The taking of Suzie and the rushed, grim violence of it all had shaken them both. They recognised Constable Leesley as the policeman who had caught them together in the tent two nights ago. This time it was Suzie who had been plucked from the streets. They could be next.

They watched a Dieppe bound ferry steaming out into the storm from the shelter of Newhaven's harbour wall. 'That's where we should be,' Matthew said.

'Another country,' said Phil, wistfully.

'Over there, across the sea, you're allowed to do it at sixteen.'

'We'd be legal.'

'Decent and proper!' Matthew announced magisterially. 'Of an age to consent!'

'One problem,' Phil said.

'Only one?'

'I get seasick.'

They watched the ferry until it had passed through the grey rain curtain that hung over the sea.

'Can you still see it?' asked Matthew.

'Yeah,' Phil lied. 'Just.'

Phil remembered how when he was little he used to watch planes so high in the sky they looked like silver pin-heads. He only knew they were there because of the vapour trails. He would watch them long after they'd gone, convinced that he could still see them. His mother told him it was bad for his eyes to stare at the sky for so long, so he became a secret plane watcher. One day she bought him a pair of polaroid sunglasses. But Phil was almost nine years old by then and had better things to do than watch the sky.

The storm blew itself out within an hour of the ferry's departure from Newhaven and, by the evening, a stillness, light and wickedly calming, had crept across the shoreline like the fingers of a cunning seducer. The rocks blossomed and the cliff faces glowed a soft ochre. Even the seagulls sang. It was the coming of a false spring; the peace after the storm, whose eye hadn't been plucked but poked with a sharp stick of its own making.

Matthew pushed Phil onto his back and unbuttoned his shirt. Then he loosened his trousers and pulled them unceremoniously down his legs. Phil neither helped nor resisted.

As Matthew stood over him and unbuckled his belt, Phil turned his head away and pressed his cheek into the ground. There was a ragged beauty in Phil's nakedness: his trousers were a soft shackle around his ankles; the unbuttoned shirt, spread open across his chest, was as a rip revealing a promise. He shut his eyes. Phil wanted only to feel now. He wanted to feel the earth, wet and cold against his buttocks, his back and his shoulders; he wanted to feel his skin contract in the evening air. He remembered Mr Cross's sexual orientation lesson and how when he watched the rain on the classroom window it blurred his vision and distorted otherwise familiar shapes into a comforting formlessness. When Phil opened his eyes again, Matthew was stepping out of his jeans.

'Hurry up,' Phil said.

When we'd got the tent up, I wanted to go back into the town. I wanted to be in the real world again, just for a bit. I wanted to be seen with Matthew, even though it would only be by strangers. I needed to know that this was all really happening. Being somewhere where there were other people, I thought, people who were getting on with their lives, would make everything feel more real. And it wasn't as if we'd have to stay there.

'What about the Law?' Matthew asked.

'Sod the Law,' I said. 'They didn't bother with us when they got Suzie, did they?'

'That was then. They weren't after us then.'

'We'll be alright, Matthew,' I promised.

'You go.'

'Not on my own.'

'I don't mind,' he said. 'I really don't mind,' I wished he did mind. I wished he minded me going without him.

'What are you going to do?' I asked him.

'I'll wait here,' he said. So I left him there, sitting outside the tent, looking out at the sea, thinking. He did a lot of thinking, did Matthew.

This time, instead of walking along the beach, I found a track that led up one of the cliffs. Suzie was wrong about that—there was another way down to her beach. When I was about halfway up I looked back. Matthew hadn't moved. I looked back again when I was near the top, and he still hadn't moved. I thought he might have waved, but he didn't.

I used to watch him when he was on the diving-board. I'd watch him as he got ready to dive up there high in the roof of the pool. It was like looking up into another world. Then he'd jump and sort of change shape in the air before hitting the water. When he surfaced he'd shake the water out of his hair, and he'd be back with us again. It was those seconds when he was flying that made him different to the rest of us.

'Matthew!' I shouted when I'd got to the top. 'Up here! Matthew!' He couldn't have heard me, not down there. From where I was standing it was hard to tell the difference between him and the rocks.

It was still quite light when I got into Seaford. I went straight to the funfair and used up all the change I had on the games in the arcade. There were only about four of us in there, so I had a go on most of the machines.

I bought a postcard for Todd, and wrote *Having a great time!!* on the back of it. I couldn't think of anything else to say. I suppose I could have said things like *Matthew and me still in love!* or *Honeymoon going well!!!* or even something simple like *Matthew sends his love.* But I didn't. The card had a drawing on it of a fat lady with *Wish You Were Here* tattooed across her tits. I addressed it to Todd at the video shop in Egremont Street. I didn't have a stamp and it was too late to find a post office that would be open, so I shoved the card in my pocket and went for a walk along the sea-front past the place where they'd got Suzie. I wondered what had happened to her, and if she was on her way home yet.

[Suzie was a chancer who got caught, and now she was on her way back to Deptford, to Sutton Terrace, where she had worried them almost to death. She was on her way back to Pete, the heart-broken tart, who was going to have to break Elizabeth's heart.

In the end, Suzie would pay dearly for her eight weeks. But not yet. First would come the welcoming tears and her parents' rash forgiveness; there would be poor cousin Elizabeth's crushed smile to contend with, and Pete's embarrassed 'Hi'. Family and friends would be falling over each other to make a star of Suzie. And Suzie would get crushed in the rush.]

I felt bad about Suzie. But if we'd let her stay with us, maybe she'd still be around. Sod her, I thought, she wasn't our problem. What happened to Suzie was going to happen anyway. Sooner or later she'd have had to go home. We were all going to have to go home, sooner or later. Anything else was crazy. That was it, I thought. Either you went back home or you became another person. You would have to become this person who didn't have a home anymore, or a past, or any of it.

You died, Phil supposed.

Matthew was standing at the water's edge watching the surf curl around his feet. He thought about the cat at home and how it tip-toed round his mother's ankles when she filled its bowl. Each small wave brought with it another chill sensation. He stood there until his feet were numb. Then he took off his trousers and walked into the sea until the water covered his knees. When the cold had numbed his legs, Matthew took off his shirt and threw it to the beach. Naked now, he walked out until the water was up to his neck. Here he would stay, he decided, until Phil returned.

'Yes, young man?' the landlord smirked, making it quite clear that he knew Phil was under age. Phil ordered a half pint of lager. 'Sixty pence,' said the landlord.

He paid for the drink and carried his glass to a table in one of the darker and more anonymous corners of the bar. He didn't recognise the woman who fed the neon-purple juke-box, which was playing a Cliff Richard record. Nor did he recognise the other woman and the three men who sat at the table by the door.

The woman from the juke-box went back to her seat and whispered to the men. They eyed Phil with the tired malevolence of bored executioners. Phil saw they were watching him and he felt a rush of panic. It was the bowel turning fear he remembered feeling in the school playground when, as a first year, he was regularly smacked about by a spiky-haired bastard called Ashworth, who was later killed in a powerboat accident. Phil secretly celebrated when he heard the news, and hoped that the death was as messy and as gruesome as they said it was. The women, titillated by their men's serious mischief, smiled grimly.

Phil finished his drink and stared at the empty glass. He wanted to leave the pub and get back to Matthew. If he left then, he would have had to walk past the table by the door. He got out Todd's postcard and read it over and over again, hoping they would go before he did.

He had to do something ordinary and everyday to unhook himself from the steely attentions of the three men and the two women who had him cornered. There was a pay-phone in the pub. Ten paces was all it would have taken, no more than five seconds away and Phil could have been dialling Sharon's number. The phone would have rung all those miles away in London. Phil thought Sharon was probably watching television (his mother certainly was) and he wished he had a paper to see what was on. He wouldn't have had to talk to Sharon. That was the beauty of the telephone. If, when he heard her voice, his nerve failed him, he could hang up. He put the postcard back in his pocket and sorted through his change (just in case). There was enough there for a conversation. Enough even for an argument, he thought. He looked across at the danger that waited at the table by the door and knew he had to make a move.

Phil got up and went into the gents. It was a clean affair with pungently-scented blue fresheners spread along the trough. The tiled walls generated a chill that, for a moment, cooled his sense of foreboding. He peed.

It took no more than five minutes in the water before the numbness turned to pain. Shivering and aching with the cold, Matthew ran out of the sea and across the beach, gathering his clothes as he went. Once he had dried off and dressed, he began to worry about Phil. He remembered that he hadn't eaten anything that day and hoped that Phil would bring something back. Anything would do, even a packet of crisps or a bar of chocolate. He should have said something. He should have given him a shopping list, he thought.

He crawled out of the tent and looked up at the cliff top. If Phil had been there, or if he had been on his way down to the beach, Matthew wouldn't have seen him. Not that night. He searched the sky for the moon and all he could find was a hint of silver that winked and teased through cracks in the cloud. And yet the sea sparkled as though it had its own secret source of light to reflect.

'Shit,' Matthew groaned. The thought of food, or rather the memory of it, made him homesick. He knew that he would never go back. He was fifteen when he started to feel the gap grow between him and his parents. Even then he had an inkling that one day he would have to leave, and not for the usual reasons: college, work, marriage. His friends were going through the same small alienaitons at home, but in their case it was simply part of growing up. They would, sooner or later, replicate their parents in themselves. Matthew knew two years ago that he would never complete the pattern. He also knew that there was nothing wrong with him. Somehow he was spared that agony.

There he was on a strange beach looking for the moon in a sky that was as foreign to him as the sea. The city, though still reverberating through his head, was beginning to recede. It was as though he was standing in the stern of an ocean- going liner watching harbour lights fade in the distance. The tastes, the smells, the sounds of the land he was leaving behind were still with him, but he knew that, like the lights, they would become nothing more than a memory. He was almost happy, and incredibly hungry.

'Shit.' He cupped his hands around his mouth, 'Phil!' he yelled.

11

Phil came out of the toilets and walked quickly across the bar and past the table at the door. He could hear laughter from the pub as the street door swung slowly shut behind him. Phil paused for a moment to get his bearings then headed for the sea-front. He would walk along the beach to get back to Matthew, he decided. It was too dark for the cliff track.

The three men and the two women from the pub drained their glasses and hurried out.

'Slags,' the landlord said. 'Why do I bother?'

The regular shrugged and pushed his jug forward for a refill. 'Because you care, Paul, that's why. Anything on the telly tonight?'

'Never watch it,' the landlord said as he handed the regular his pint.

It was then that Constable Leesley came into the pub. If he had the time, and if he happened to be passing, he would call into the local pubs on his evening shift. He knew that pubs were both the start and the finish of many an illegal adventure. Drugs changed hands in pubs; plots were hatched, information bought, sold and part-exchanged. On a cold night Leesley might even be tempted to a quick short. 'Everything alright?' he asked.

Phil hurried along the beach. He had to force his way through the shingle and the sand and, though every step was an effort, he felt a lightness about him. The escape from the pub had come like the release from Suzie, home, school and Sharon.

A light swept across his face, moved along the beach, then returned to dazzle him. He froze as still as a rabbit in a poacher's flashlight.

'Stay there,' a woman's voice called through the dark. He heard footsteps coming up behind him, crunching through the shingle. 'Stay there,' the woman repeated. The light remained on his face. There must be at least two of them, he thought, one holding the torch and the woman who called to him. There would have been no point in trying to make a run for it.

'What's going on?' Phil turned to where he thought the woman was.

'Just a bit of fun,' she said as she moved into the light. He recognized her as one of the women from the pub. She was the one who was feeding the juke-box.

'I'm late,' Phil said. 'I've got to go.' He started to walk away. The woman grabbed him by the arm and spun him round. The light went off and he heard more footsteps coming towards him. When the torch flashed on again, he saw they were all there, the two women and the three men from the pub. Fear stirred in his bowels.

'We know all about you,' one of the men said.

'Know what?' Phil asked.

'You and your mate. We know all about you.'

'And we're going to show you what you're missing,' a woman's voice chimed. The torch moved across to the woman from the juke-box and played on her as if it were a spotlight.

'I don't think so,' she said. 'It's too bloody cold.'

'Do it,' the man with the torch ordered. Then the woman undressed, quickly and without ceremony. Another of the men moved up behind her and started to fondle her breasts. He pushed her to within inches of Phil. 'Make you want to throw up, does it?' he asked.

Phil could see that the woman was making a pretence of enjoying the game. Maybe she loved the man who was touching her, and maybe she wished it could be different.

Romance.

He thought how ugly they looked. 'I don't know what all this is supposed to be about,' he said, keeping the fear out of his voice.

'Remember Suzie?' the man with the torch asked.

'Yes, I remember Suzie,' said Phil.

'She warned us. She told us you were a couple of shirt-lifters.'

'Bollocks,' Phil said. A fist smashed into the side of his head. He tasted blood in his mouth.

'We thought we'd try to cure you,' Phil heard another male voice hiss through the ringing in his head. 'We thought we might convert you to Christianity and the English way of life.'

Phil put a hand to his lips and felt the blood on his fingers. He spat at the ground and caught the naked woman's legs with the spray. The men laughed and Phil went cold. They could kill him, he thought, and it wouldn't mean much until the morning, when the alcohol had thinned.

'AIDS,' he whispered, shoving his blood-stained hand into the torch-light.

The naked woman looked down at her legs. 'Shine the light. Shine the light!' she screamed. The light moved and she saw the red pattern across her thighs. 'Fuck,' she said and ran towards the sea. 'Fuck it. Fuck it. Fuck it!'

Phil backed away. 'Risk it if you like. Take a chance. Go on.' He spat towards them. They jumped back.

'You bastard. You filthy bastard,' he heard one of the men shout. He couldn't see them anymore, just the light from their torch bobbing further and further away into the night. And then they were gone and Phil felt truly alone.

Though it was a calm night, the sea howled, the wind screamed and the shingle beneath his feet roared with every step he took. The adrenalin was still racing.

He saw car headlights flash across the sky from the sea-front and instinctively threw himself to the ground. As he lay there he heard a car door slam, and then he heard footsteps above him on the promenade. A powerful beam of light moved along the beach away from where Phil was lying.

'Anybody there?' a voice called. He didn't recognise it as belonging to any of the men from the pub. 'It's the police,' the voice shouted.

Leesley was on the promenade searching the beach with his flashlight for a victim of violence. The landlord in the pub had warned him that something might happen that night. He'd read the signs and he was rarely wrong, the landlord told him. Hadn't he, after all, put him on to Suzie?

Phil didn't move a muscle. He hugged the shingle as a drowning man might hug a piece of flotsam. He would go wherever the shingle took him.

'If you're down there, stand in the light and let me see you.' Leesley called. The beam of light shone directly over where Phil was lying and caught the naked woman, who was still frantically washing her thighs at the water's edge.

'Don't move,' Leesley called to her.

Then Phil stood up and found the light. Leesley could see the blood around Phil's mouth. 'What's been going on?' he asked.

Phil pointed to the woman. 'Ask her,' he said.

The woman continued to rub neurotically at her legs. 'Well?' Leesley shouted.

'A bit of fun, that's all,' she said. She made fists of her hands and was now pummelling her thighs.

'It was supposed to be a bit of fun, that's all.' She turned to Phil. 'Bastard!' she screamed. She aimed all the venom and hatred and spite and fear that had haunted and dogged her for most of her twenty-five years at Phil. 'Fucking bastard!'

Phil shrugged. As long as he had blood in his mouth, he was untouchable. 'They beat me up, officer,' Phil said calmly. He spat blood again.

Constable Leesley began to feel uneasy. Here he was confronted by a bleeding boy and a naked woman, fear and loathing caught in his torch-light. A nightful of crime, surely. If he climbed down to the beach, they could make a run for it. He couldn't go back to the car to radio for assistance, there was no guarantee that either of them would be there when he returned. He was as trapped as they were, more so if anyone cared to test it.

The woman made off along the water's edge. Leesley swung the light round and caught her in the beam. 'Don't move,' he yelled. She stopped in her tracks, as though trapped in the beam. Phil ran. Leesley didn't stand a chance and had to make do with the naked woman, whom he later charged with behaviour likely to offend public decency. When the full story emerged, the charges were dropped by an understanding Inspector. He felt that any press coverage of the case would be more likely to offend the sensibilities of the public than the crime itself had done. The protagonists were, after all, a couple of tarts, three drunks and a homosexual. The scene was a lonely beach on a dark night. No decency was actually offended against.

12

Suzie had told them about Phil and Matthew. There was no malice in the telling. It was an act of self-preservation, nothing more sinister than that.

It happened the night Matthew and Phil had left her outside the pub. The bar was crowded and when Suzie came into the pub she didn't see the men, who were sitting at a table by the door to the ladies. They bullied her into sitting with them and teased her about her new friends.

'They're just a couple of pooves,' she told them. 'They're on their honeymoon, so they're hardly going to be interested in me, are they?' She hoped that this would keep the men amused and off her back. She hoped also that her dismissal of Phil and Matthew might earn her a few points and that, just until she could get away, the men might treat her better.

She let them buy her a drink, then she escaped through the fire exit in the ladies' toilets.

When Phil got back to Matthew, he found him in the tent wrapped in his sleeping bag.

'Where have you been?' Matthew asked sulkily.

'And have you got anything to eat? Where the hell have you been, Phil? I'm starving.'

Phil told him. Then Matthew took him to the sea, where he helped him wash the blood from his mouth. They went back to the tent and made love. Matthew was gentle and Phil loved him all the more for that.

The next morning we walked to Newhaven. I didn't much fancy going back into Seaford. We left the tent where it was, we thought we'd risk it, and just took our bags with us. Matthew wanted to hitch, but I said I'd rather walk and, as I was the one with the sore mouth, he agreed.

When we got to Newhaven we went straight into a supermarket and bought a cooked chicken and a loaf of bread, which we ate sitting on a bench overlooking a beach. We stuffed ourselves until we both felt ill, then we went down to the beach, stretched out on the sand and went to sleep.

Matthew was still sleeping when I woke. I watched him for a bit and thought about when we made love after he'd helped me clean up and how it all began to make sense again: us being here together, leaving London, just being free. I thought about how much I loved him. I remembered the face of the woman when the bloke was playing with her tits, and I wondered about Sharon.

I shook Matthew awake. 'I'm going to have a look around,' I told him. He said he'd wait for me there and then he shut his eyes and went back to sleep again.

That morning, Sharon decided against school. She wasn't feeling up to it and that was that. She'd tried all night to hate Phil. It was both reasonable and understandable that she should attempt to manipulate her emotions in this way. Phil had hurt her deeply. He had and was continuing to humiliate her. Because of Phil, she had lost her self confidence and was beginning to lose her grip on what she understood to be reality. Her reality had been punched through by Phil's desertion. Phil was a bastard. Vera was right about him.

'However much I think he's nice, Sharon,' Vera had told her, 'You've got to admit he's a bastard.'

Vera was alright now. Things were going well for her. Dennis had phoned and they'd arranged to go out together. They were going to give it a try.

'And what about Dennis?' Sharon asked Vera.

'I reckon he'll turn out to be a bastard an' all,' Vera said. 'But then again he might not,' she added.

However hard she tried, though, Sharon could not bring herself to truly hate Phil. 'You can't just stop loving someone,' she said. 'Not just like that.'

'Not just like what?' Vera asked.

'Like suddenly. Not just like that. Like overnight.' Sharon explained.

'No,' Vera agreed. 'But they don't half find it

easy to stop loving you. And if it ain't overnight, it's the next morning. D'you now what I mean?'

So that night, armed with Vera's common sense, Sharon went to bed determined to wake up sensible and cured and no longer hurting. She cried herself to sleep and by the morning she knew that she would rather die than face another day without Phil.

Then the phone rang.

The first thing I did when I left Matthew sleeping on the beach was to look for the post office so that I could send Todd his card. There was a phone there and I called Sharon.

'Hello?' she said.

'It's me,' I told her. 'Phil.'

'Phil?'

'That's right. How are you?'

'Phil?'

'Yes.'

'Where are you?'

'Newhaven,' I said. 'Where the ferries are.'

'Are you going away?' she asked.

'No.'

'Then what are you doing at the ferries?'

'We're just looking around.'

'Phil?'

'What?'

'I miss you,' she said. 'I love you, Phil.'

'I love you an' all.'

'Promise?'

'Come on, Sharon.'

'Is he with you?'

'Who?'

'Matthew. You know who.'

'No. He's asleep on the beach.'

'Phil?'

'What?'

'I want you to come back,' she said. Then she started to cry. 'I don't know what to say to my friends,' she said. 'I feel such an idiot, Phil.'

'Tell them to sod off.'

'I'm not going in to school today.'

'Why not?'

'I can't face it. I don't want to do anything any more,' she said. 'I don't even want to go out. And Vera's seeing Dennis.'

'Dennis? From school?'

'Yes, Dennis.'

'Why Dennis?'

'Why her?' she said.

'Bloody hell. Dennis is a prat.'

'I feel a prat, Phil.'

'Why?'

'You know why.'

'I'm sorry, okay?'

'No, it's not bloody okay. What are we going to do?'

'I don't know, do I?' I said. 'What do you mean what are we going to do, anyway?'

'About us. What are we going to do?'

'What do you want to do?'

'I want to see you.'

'It's a bit difficult.'

'Why?'

'You know why.'

'No, I don't.'

'Sharon, you know why.'

'I just want to see you, Phil, that's all. Why can't I see you? You're cruel, you know that?'

'I'm not cruel, Sharon,' I said.

'You're a bastard, then.'

'I'm not, Sharon.'

'Vera reckons you are.'

'Tell Vera to fuck off, then'

'She reckons you're all bastards.'

'Slag.'

'Phil?'

'What?'

'I want to see you. Even if that's it. Even if it's for the last time. Even if we finish it. I want to see you. Please.'

'No.'

'Why not?'

'You know why not, Sharon.'

Matthew was awake when Phil returned to the beach. 'Alright?' he asked.

'Yes. You?'

'I've been thinking about Suzie,' Matthew said.

'Nothing to do with us,' Phil interrupted. 'Don't get involved, that's the rule. Remember?

'What do you think's happened to her?'

'I don't care. I don't give a shit what happens to her.'

'I thought you liked her.'

'I did,' Phil said. 'I don't want to become like her, though.'

'We won't be like Suzie. No chance.'

'Matthew, I made a phone call.'

'We're here because we want to be here. Nothing's keeping us. Just us.'

'I phoned Sharon.'

'We're better off here,' Matthew continued.

'I needed to talk to her.'

'Fancy a swim?' Matthew got to his feet and started to undress.

'She's coming down tomorrow.'

'Then what?' Matthew asked angrily.

Phil sighed. 'I don't know,' he said. 'We'll see, yeah?'

13

Vera saw Sharon off at the station. 'Good luck,' she yelled as she waved the train away from the platform.

Vera and Sharon had spent the morning shopping. This was it. Sharon was going to get her man back, and she had to look good. The better she looked, the better she felt. Sharon felt wonderful as she settled back in her seat. She was nervous and excited and knew exactly what she was going to say. This was to be a meeting of forgiveness. Recriminations could come later.

Within twenty minutes of hearing the good news, Vera was round at Sharon's house. They hugged and they kissed and they danced a little dance in the small hall.

'I can't believe it, Vera,' Sharon screamed. 'He wants me to go down and see him.'

'You see that you bring him back with you, that's all,' Vera cautioned. 'Once you get your hands on him, don't let him go.'

'I won't,' Sharon promised.

'Remember, he's a worm.'

'I know.'

'Well don't forget, that's all.'

'I'm so happy, Vera.'

'What are you going to wear, then?' Vera asked.

'I don't know.' Sharon began to panic. 'I've only got what he's seen me in. I've got to get something different to wear, right? Something special.'

'Why not?' agreed Vera. 'Treat yourself. I would.'

So they arranged to go shopping together the next morning.

Phil was waiting on the platform at Seaford station when the train pulled in. He waved to Sharon as she stepped out of the carriage. Don't run, she said to herself. Let him wait a bit longer.

They kissed briefly and then they walked arm in arm through the barrier and out of the station building into the street. Sharon was shaking. Her stomach was alive with butterflies. They walked to the junction in silence. Neither wanted to be the first to speak.

'So,' they said simultaneously. Sharon laughed. 'You go first,' she offered.

'I don't know what to say,' said Phil.

'You could say you were pleased to see me.'

'You know I am.'

'Say it, then.'

'I am pleased to see you, Sharon.'

'And that you've missed me?'

'You know I've missed you.'

'Tell me then. Tell me you've missed me.'

'I've missed you.'

She kissed him on the cheek as they ran across the road. She noticed the swelling around Phil's mouth and the bruise that spread from his ear to his jaw. 'What happened?' she asked touching his face.

'I had a bit of an accident,' Phil said.

'What happened?'

'I'll tell you later.'

'Does it hurt?'

'Not exactly.'

'Poor baby.' She kissed him again, ever so gently, on the side of his face that ached.

When they got to the front, Sharon just wanted to stand there, look out to sea and breathe in the air. 'It's beautiful,' she remarked. 'I couldn't live here, but it's beautiful to come and look at it, isn't it?'

Phil told her that he thought it was all very special.

'Could you live here?' she asked. 'I mean for ever.'

'Yes.'

'I couldn't. The noise would drive me crazy. It never stops, does it?' she said. Phil realised that he'd already become so accustomed to the sound of the sea he no longer noticed it. It had become part of the landscape. It was as though the air was alive.

'What about London?' he asked her.

'It's all going somewhere in London, isn't it?'

'Yes.' Phil didn't want to argue. There wasn't, after all, anything to argue about. Maybe, if their roles were reversed, he would have felt the same way about it as Sharon did.

Whilst he was waiting at the station for Sharon's train to arrive he was almost decided on going back to London with her. He missed home. He knew he would miss Matthew. But whilst he was with him, whilst he knew that Matthew was waiting for him, that he was on the beach, their beach, waiting; whilst he knew that Matthew would be there when he got back, he could not, no matter how hard he tried, imagine the pain of missing Matthew. It was just a jumble of words and remembered emotions to Phil. *Missing. Wanting. Dreaming. Feeling. Crying. I miss you. I miss you, I miss you.* What was really missing was the pain. He knew about it, but he couldn't feel it. He missed Sharon (and he felt it) because she wasn't there. He missed his mother (and he felt that) because she wasn't there.

'We ought to move,' he said to Sharon.

She slipped an arm through his and let him lead her away along the promenade.

'You haven't said anything about what I'm wearing,' she gently reproached. 'I spent all morning shopping for it.'

'It's very nice.'

'Vera helped me choose. Do you really like it?'

'Yes.'

'I'll tell her. She'll be pleased. She was so happy, you would have thought it was her who was coming down, not me.'

Romance, thought Phil.

Sharon suddenly stopped walking. She pulled

Phil round to face her. 'I don't want to see him,' she said. 'We don't have to see him, do we? I'm really sorry, Phil, but I don't want to see him.'

'Why not?'

'I don't know. Maybe I'm jealous.'

'I want you to like him, Sharon.'

'You're kidding.'

'No I'm not. I want you to like Matthew. It's important.'

'I don't even want to see him, sod liking him.

'All my stuff's down there.'

'Well I ain't staying or nothing.'

'What did you come down for then?'

'To see my feller,' she said, 'That's why. To have a day out with him. And to sort him out. Because I love you.'

Matthew had taken down the tent and was rolling it up when Phil and Sharon arrived.

'You got here then?' was what Matthew said when he saw Sharon.

'Hello, Matthew,' she said.

I watched them as they tried to suss each other out. All of a sudden I felt sorry for her. She shouldn't have been there. I felt a rush of love for her. I wanted to put my arms around her and cuddle her and send her back home.

She asked Matthew what had happened to my face.

'He got beaten up. For being a poof. Didn't he tell you?'

'No,' she said. 'As it happens, he didn't.'

'Well that's what happens. If you're a poof.'

I wanted to send her back where she belonged, where she understood everything; where everything was as she understood it to be. I wanted Matthew to be nice to her. I wanted him to like her and to be kind to her. She didn't belong with us. Sitting there on a rock in her new clothes, Sharon was a visitor, someone we should have been polite to. And there she was trying to work it all out. I felt sorry for her.

'Sharon looked me over. 'Is that true?' she asked me. 'Is that really what happened.'

'Yes,' I said.

'Why didn't you tell me about it?'

'I said I'd tell you later.'

'You said you had an accident.'

'I lied, Sharon,' I said.

Matthew knew that Phil was thinking of leaving him and going back to London with Sharon. Phil had already told him as much.

Whatever Phil chose to do, Phil and Sharon, the relationship, was over. It had ended in the cafeteria at the swimming pool. They could probably have dragged it out for a few more weeks, months even, but as a relationship with a future it was over. It was as dead as a headless chicken.

Matthew didn't dislike Sharon, and, unlike hers, his emotions were not cluttered by the need to compete for Phil's affections. And though his wasn't a possessive love, he did not want to lose Phil.

Matthew wanted Sharon to say that she understood (or at least to pretend that she understood—he had no great expectations of Sharon)—and to return to London alone. He wanted her to shock them both (and herself) by telling them that she understood. He wouldn't have minded a lie. He didn't want or expect her blessings, nor did he expect her to wish them a happy ever after. He merely wanted her to go away, to leave them to their simplicity and to get on with hers.

Phil and Matthew were learning. They were learning how to survive their sexuality in a world of senseless punches and mindless (and sometimes cynical) persecution. And every day it became a little harder to achieve the ordinariness that heterosexuals took for granted.

Matthew wanted Sharon to leave them alone. If Phil was going to go with her, then he wanted them both to leave him alone.

'What are you going to do?' Sharon asked him.

'Hang about. I don't know yet.'

'Come back with us,' Sharon offered. It was a polite offer that she knew would be refused.

Matthew turned to Phil, who looked uncomfortable. 'You're going back then, are you?'

Phil shrugged. He didn't know what he was going to do. Going back was just that: going back. There is always a measure of safety in reversal. He knew what was there. Going back was a seductive thought. It would also be a death. But Phil didn't yet know enough about deaths and reversals, nor did Matthew, or Sharon for that matter.

'I've got to lie if I go back home,' Matthew explained. 'I've got to worry about other people's feelings while they slag me off. I've got to care about people who don't give a shit about me.'

'That's because you're different. It's always hard when you're different,' Sharon said. 'They know about you back home, don't they? They know you're different.'

'Know what?' Phil asked, irritated by Sharon's sudden grasp of the problem.

'That he's different.'

'Unnatural,' said Matthew.

'Weird,' Phil said.

Sharon was out of the game.

'A nancy-boy.'

'Bent.'

'Gay.'

'Happy.' Phil sprang to his feet and ran down to the beach. He held out his arms in an open embrace. 'Beware dangerous deviants!' he shouted.

Matthew ran to join him and together they danced into the sea.

Sharon watched them from her rock. She wished she had the nerve to run in with them. She wished she wasn't wearing her new clothes. She couldn't get these clothes wet, not yet, she'd only worn them once.

14

Matthew watched Phil and Sharon clamber over the rocks towards the cliff path. It was early evening and the sky, though still light, was flecked with wisps of red and pink from a slow sunset.

The fact that Phil had chosen to go back with Sharon came as no great surprise to any of them. Matthew accepted it, Sharon expected it, and Phil fell in line with what he thought was the inevitable.

Matthew had decided to spend one more night there under the cliffs. Tomorrow he would move on. He unrolled the tent and started to pitch it.

Phil waved from the top of the cliff, but Matthew had stopped watching them as soon as they had started up the path.

By the time he had put up the tent, Matthew knew that the adventure was over. Sharon and Phil were on their way to the railway station. Suzie was probably home by now. Her betrayal of them was forgivable, it was all part of the adventure.

It could have worked out, Matthew thought. They had been together for less than a week, but he knew it could have worked.

They would have moved on together. They would have found odd-jobs (Romance) to keep them going and eventually, before the winter, they would have settled somewhere they both fancied. In time they would have made new friends and their new life would have become their only life.

Romance.

As Phil and Sharon approached the railway station, Sharon tried to hurry Phil along. 'Come on,' she pleaded, 'or we'll miss the train. I want to go home, Phil.'

'We'll be alright,' he said. 'We've got plenty of time.'

'I don't want to risk it.'

'We'll be alright.'

'You want to stay, don't you?' she said.

'Don't be daft. I'm here aren't I?'

'Phil.'

'What?'

'Kiss me.'

Phil put his arms around her and kissed her.

'I love you,' she said. 'I really love you.' Sharon had got her man. He was with her, he had his arms around her and she could still taste his mouth. They were on their way back to London; back to Vera, to school, to the Spread Eagle and Dennis and the queer feller from the bar. For a moment, but only for a moment, the thought of returning to all of that filled her with dread. 'You want to stay, don't you?' she said again. If he'd only say yes, she thought, if he'd say it now, she would understand.

Not about Matthew, she didn't ever want to understand about Matthew, but if Phil didn't want to go back she would understand. *Say it now! Say it now! Say it now!* She wanted to scream it at him. Sometimes she hated him. She really did hate him. She hated his weakness because it made her feel weak; she hated his softness because it drained her of resolve; she hated his confusion because it threatened her tomorrows; and, more than anything, she hated loving him because it made her lonely.

'You alright?' Phil asked her.

'I won't cry anymore. I promise.'

'Me neither,' Phil said.

The closer we got to the station, the more edgy I began to feel. This really was going back, in every way. I wondered what Matthew was doing. I knew he was going to stay another night. I liked that thought. I liked it because I could picture where he was. I could see him there.

Sharon hadn't changed, nor had I. I still felt the same way about things. Nothing would have changed at home either. It wasn't home that was the problem, though, it was everything else. School would smell the same as it always did.

And Sharon was the same as she always was. It wasn't her fault her voice sounded the same as it always did. She couldn't help the way she was. It wasn't her fault that kissing her tasted the same as it always did, or that her body felt the way it always felt. None of it was her fault. I loved her for all that. It used to turn me on. I thought it was sexy. I used to get nervous about seeing her, and dream about touching her. None of it was Sharon's fault.

I was going back to a sodding great hole left by Matthew. And I didn't fancy it. None of it.

15

Matthew had settled for missing Phil. He knew it was going to hurt, especially at night.

He had already decided that he would not try to stop thinking of Phil. There would be no point in trying. There would be plenty of time for that later. Once he had moved on, there would plenty of time to lay the ghosts. That night he needed the mourning. He would remember the fun, the good times, the excitement. He would remember how it felt to have Phil close to him, to hear him sleeping, to feel him wake. The memories were still fresh enough to be real.

He would think of Phil, and maybe Phil would think of him. Once he'd moved on it was possible that they would never see each other again. Phil would never find him, and he wouldn't go looking for Phil. With new landscapes, the memories would fade or, rather, the pain would go away and the memories would remain. He didn't want to forget any of it, ever.

Matthew stripped off and walked down to the sea. He knew the water would be icy, and that was what he wanted to feel against his skin.

When the water had reached his waist, Matthew

heard a shout. He looked round and his soul sang. There, at the top of the cliff, was Phil.

'Matthew!' Phil called, waving his arms above his head.

'What happened?' Matthew shouted.

'I came back, didn't I?'

'Jump!'

Phil ran down the track as fast as he dared, and Matthew came out of the water to meet him.

ROMANCE